Deathstar Voyage

IAN WALLACE

Deathstar Voyage

a downtime mystery cruise

London
Dennis Dobson

Conjointly
to my wife's wristwatch
and to mine

First published in Great Britain in 1972
by Dobson Books Ltd, 80 Kensington Church Street, London W8 4BZ
Printed in Great Britain by Straker Brothers Ltd., Whitstable
ISBN 0 234 77498 3

FORENOTE

There is nothing intentionally topical in *Deathstar Voyage;* no element is introduced for any purpose other than those of story and character development; and all fictitious geographical and planetary names were chosen solely for their odd or otherwise pleasant flavor in the author's taste. There is no direct or indirect reference to real individuals in *Deathstar Voyage;* and all personal names and descriptions were generated for interest, for convenience, or at random. I did steal some of the background color from literary reflections of the nineteenth-century British Raj.

For certain indispensable services, I wish here to express my gratitude to (in alpha order) Steven Frimmer, Marcia Magill, Mavis McIntosh, and Elizabeth McKee.

Vash, 1969   IAN WALLACE

Part One

FROLIC STREET

I

Her hand lightly hooked on the crook'd arm of the tall, tweedy, big-shouldered king, Claudine literally danced beside him, looking eagerly this way and that, her tiny feet interweaving in counterpoint to his leisurely stride; and in full dignified response to her delight, his eyes gleamed and his heavy white mustachios curled upward above his majestic white beard. Claudine peered at assorted passersby, swung her handbag recklessly, chortled at little street-accidents, gaped at the bizarre wares displayed in the sidewalk marts of Frolic Street. Every so often she stopped dead to point upward at the splendid stars that glowed naked in the black space-blanket, burning through the low glow of the gaslit avenue; for kilometer-long Frolic Street constituted the entire length of the transparently roof-plated top deck in the port hull of the starship *Eiland of Ligeria*.

It was their first afternoon out—call it night, because of the stars—and they were in no hurry, and they made slow progress: the many hundreds of others on the narrow street were mostly in the same gay holiday mood, they kept being bumped and didn't mind. For Claudine —and even for the king, who for once wasn't on display —it was the nearest thing to a holiday for a long while, and it was going to last a week.

They wandered in shop after shop, all of them wide-open sidewalk shops, some shallow, some deep and bright, some deep and dim: shriveled odoriferous spices hanging from ceilings, infinitely intricate laces, a bizarre

9

assortment of clocks and watches and cigars and miscellaneous complicated fine-mechanical gimcracks, a multi-tinkling den of music boxes, a diamondry with real diamonds (all costly, no fakes), a sidewalk café, a go-go theater, a music museum with period instruments ranging from a Greek cithara of the seventh century B.C. to an Aldebaranian zassou of the twenty-second century A.D., a stand of Ligerian mountebanks, a sidewalk café . . . This one they paused at, and the king ordered zacs, and Claudine slipped off her shoes and sipped, watching people.

Her gay smile suddenly froze—it didn't change, it just became an immobile smile. Then, bringing her zac-glass close to her lips, she said softly: "Flirt with me, Your Majesty—and while you're at it, tell me who is standing behind me."

Playing up splendidly, the king leaned forward, laid a hand on her hand on the tabletop, and whispered: "Only a portly dowager who has lost something and is worriedly hunting through her bag for it. I've never seen her before."

Claudine set down the glass and laid her small brown hand atop the large, fine, white, gnarl-veined hand of the king. She said: "I felt a woman there. I sensed her concern and heard no sound. That was all."

His hand tightened on hers. "Can't you be off duty? A moment ago, you were so happy—"

"I still am," she assured him, and her large, dark, glowing eyes backed it up. "This is delicious duty, Your Majesty. However, it is duty, and I wish to do it while I am enjoying it. It would be rough if you got plunked."

Sighing semicomically, the king withdrew his hand from her hands—they did not restrain him. Using a small silver electronic lighter to kindle a long cigar—long enough for beard safety, and then some—he told the matchflame: "I am only sixty-one, and I could wish that the duty to me were unlimited."

This time Claudine reached over and took his hand and squeezed it. "I am only twenty-seven," she told him, "and so could I. But since it must be limited, I want it to

10

be like wonderful poetry—squeezing extra delight out of its very restrictions."

The king inhaled cigar smoke, exhaled through his nose like a fire dragon, and told her candidly: "The dowager is gone, and so is my instant of niddering flame, and I am wholly the dignified monarch, and tonight there will be no need for you to lock the door between our communicating rooms. However, a night may come when *I* will lock it."

Her lips came together and her grin went wicked. "Then I will never disturb you by knocking, I will only quietly try the door, and if it is locked, it is locked. You are the king, but also you are a man, and one of my duties is discretion." And she could not resist a little probe: "Tell me—does your queen treat you with equal consideration?"

He contemplated her gravely. "There is no queen. We do not marry."

"Oh?"

"You do not know my Ligeria?"

"Not yet."

"It is a fascinating planet, with its beautiful white sun Altair. It is much like Earth in its composition; and like Earth also in the sense that it has several major races of different skin-colors. Our white race has been the ruling race for several centuries, and my immediate bloodline for several generations. But because the majority on our planet have golden skins, and because the golds take what is to us whites a peculiar view of marriage, we kings avoid protocol complications by not marrying at all."

Her eyes narrowed. "And yet you mentioned your bloodline."

"From time to time," he told her blandly, "my path crosses the path of an aristocratic white woman. When I choose, or when I die, it is for me or for my Regency Board to designate my successor from among such young candidates as these women may wish to present."

Her lips were pursed. She murmured: "I like the bouquet of your cigar. I notice that the cigar is not banded."

"They are made for me. Thank you."

11

"And what is it about the marriage customs of your golden people that necessitates the felicity of these arrangements?"

"They are matriarchal and polyandrous. Were I to marry, they would regard me as merely a disposable consort for my queen—my *eiland*. As it is, my status puzzles their semantics; I am occasionally designated *her* majesty."

They brooded.

"Linked with such a marriage procedure is a bizarre outlook on funerals," the king added. "The ritual I have in mind is rather like your East Indian *suttee* in reverse: we call it *bradzh*."

"Bradzh," she repeated, savoring the broad *a*. "What is it?"

"When a queen dies, all her husbands and consorts are burned with her on her funeral pyre. Alive, that is."

She fingered her zac-glass with both hands. "How wise you are, indeed, to avoid marriage!"

"The practice of *bradzh* has been illegal since my grandfather. But it happens."

She frowned. "I've noticed that a number of the crew, including a couple of officers, are golden Ligerians. Is there going to be any misunderstanding of *my* position with respect to you?"

"I think not, if you refrain from ordering me around. The people aboard are educated to our customs."

"I only want to be sure that there will be no security problem. If there is, I should know."

"Not from that. But I do think of one. If I lock our door—or if you are elsewhere—what happens to my security?"

Both her black brows went flat, and her mouth went wide and flat with the corners semi-satirically upturned a little, and she told him: "We have Chief Tuli and four yeomen of the Galactic Police, in addition to the police crew of the ship under Lieutenant Brh. There are only two doors to your suite—the main one into your private corridor, and my private entrance: to these doors only your five people and my five people and Lieutenant Brh

12

and I have keys, and I presume that all these people can be trusted—I know mine can be. Your salon has a window which cannot be opened because outside there is only space, and a ventilating system which can be electronically monitored. There will be no time when you are not covered."

One of his great white eyebrows came down. "Do you think it good tactics to make yourself unnecessary?"

Up went one of hers. "Do you think I have?"

He grinned broadly, showing fine teeth—all his own. "If your drink is done, Claudine, there's a show down the street that we ought to take in."

The theater was intimate, it seated a hundred, the king had a private box that was practically onstage, the stars were overhead. It was old-time vaudeville, featuring a succession of the best acts in the galaxy: they entered during acrobatics by trained Capellan zaguars, which were followed by an exquisite ballet of Rigelian floaternudies. The king advised Claudine, however, that the act they had really come for was the pre-finale: the Great Doré. "I am intensely interested in this young man," he observed. And presently it was time for Doré, and the curtain rose on him.

He was in midair.

Claudine caught her breath. Doré was a monster—the foulest-ugliest creature her eyes had ever been insulted by!

But he waved his hand slowly before his face—and she gasped. The Great Doré had become a golden Adonis!

Swallowing, she muttered to the king: "Strontilite mask. They're illegal."

"But light and easy," he countered. "Watch Doré."

He hovered just above her box, looking down upon her. She could see no supporting wires, nor any bulges in his clothing that could be created by antigrav equipment. (The nudies, at least, had inbuilt *natural* antigrav equipment.) On a long descending curve, Doré now floated down to the stage, alit like a feather, bowed, and went into his act.

13

It lasted half an hour. Not once did he speak, but his long arms and hands and legs and feet and his expressive face and facile head operated to music in a pantomime that advised whatever he was about to do and then signaled its triumphant accomplishment.

The things he did were simple enough. He began by producing a large rabbit from a small silk topper; deftly holding the hat on his fingertips, he balanced the rabbit upon it; abruptly, without visible motion, the hat was on the rabbit. He brought out a small chair with a table beside it; as he went to sit on the chair, suddenly the chair was on the other side of the table, and he barely saved himself from falling; he went over there to try again, and the chair instantly and without visible motion repositioned itself; finally with a grimace he gave up, waved a hand, and chair and table vanished. That brought more applause than the rabbit.

Doré went now into more spectacular *gestes*. He brought out two nudies: they stood side by side, apparently identical; he dropped a medallion about the throat of the right-hand nudie, and waved a hand, and behold: the medallion rested between the breasts of the left-hand nudie. A third nudie he summoned and posed to audience-left of the medallioned one; and the ornament was imperceptibly transferred to *it*. (Nudies were neuter.) But now came a new turn: alternately lifting the medallion and gesturing at the nudies, Doré implanted doubt in the minds of Claudine and the rest whether he was switching the medallion or switching nudies. To settle the matter, he took a stance to audience-left of the medallioned nudie; and abruptly *it* stood at *his* left—and *he* wore the medallion! As the nudies floated away, Claudine imagined that the applause was bearing them aloft.

The finale of his act was a spectacular-graceful tour de force. Doré wore an ornate powder-blue shoulder-jacket trimmed with gold, his arms were thrust through short sleeves; and as the music went gay allegro, he removed the jacket, waved it to show that it was lined with white satin trimmed with gold, and replaced it blue-side-out. As he walked in a lithe semidance about the stage, a ten-girl

14

chorus line danced out, wearing (among a minimum of other things) similar jackets of canary yellow trimmed with bronze; and these they waved in unison to show that the linings were satin-white trimmed with black. Now the brassy music went allegretto; and the girls pirouetted while Doré wove among them—his jacket, and their jackets, continually and spontaneously reversing themselves in a dizzying variety of harmonious permutations.

The curtain fell, and rose seven times: twice for all the stars of the show, twice for Doré and his chorus line, thrice more for Doré alone. During his next-last bow, smiling gaily, he double-flipped his jacket once again; at the last bow, he waved both hands in the cease-fire signal and bowed formally and low. Not again could their beating palms drive the curtain upward.

They drifted silently back up the street among the people. Claudine was not dancing: head down, she clung almost disconsolate to the arm of the king—past the sidewalk café, the Ligerian mountebanks, the music museum, the go-go theater, the sidewalk café . . .

"Pfennig for your thoughts," he finally prodded.

She looked up with a slightly pained smile. "They're assorted," she told him. "Mainly—how did he do it? Partly—who is he?"

The king spread hands. "In a way, the answers to both questions are the same answer. From his complexion, and also from his peculiar talent, one knows that he has to be a golden Ligerian."

"Then you breed very beautiful people. But how is this related to his talent?"

"Everything he did was one or another form of psychokinetic transposition. This you dig?"

"*Psychokinetic,* yes: moving physical objects by sheer mind-control. *Transposition,* yes: making two things go flip-flop. But it's the first time I've run into the combination."

"Transposition is a thing that some of our golden Ligerian mystics are very good at. They keep it a mystery, it hasn't spread through the galaxy—but Ligeria is where to

15

learn it. Doré isn't the first one who ever used it for profane purposes—but despite his youth, he is almost the best, sacred *or* profane."

"Who in the galaxy could be better than *that?*"

"It's a long story that I will tell you some time in the privacy of my salon. By the way—talking of origins— what's *yours?*"

Her smile went gay again; her white teeth were wonderful against her light mahogany skin. "I am told that five continents on three planets collaborated in my design. Anyhow, I was unveiled in Marseilles. So natch, I became a cop, which was one of two obvious possibilities—"

The king broke in: "I still want to know, much as I enjoy it, why I had a cop assigned to me on what is supposed to be a pleasure cruise to my own home planet. What's the point, Claudine—when they tell me I'm the most beloved monarch who ever ruled Ligeria?"

She explained again, patiently, lightly: "You were our guest on Earthworld: we guarded you there. You're going home now, so you get our guarding all the way."

"But I don't *need* guarding—"

With her left hand Claudine thrust her handbag in front of his chest; something hit the bag, *chid;* her right hand released his arm, snaked into her bosom, whipped out an electronic gun, fired oblique right—all in a silent second, leaving her standing with crossed arms. She frowned. Bringing the gun to her lips, she blew three soft fluting notes on a tiny tube at its breach: nobody even turned around. Dropping the little gun into its nest, bringing her handbag down to her side, she engaged the arm of the paralyzed king. "Come here," she told him. "I want to show you something."

She led him to the door of the watch-and-clock shop which had display counters outside. A small cluster of shocked people was gathering behind one of the counters: this counter was glass-paned, and its framing was rather grotesquely enameled with alternating stripes of white and gold, and its contents were, grotesquely at a watch-and-clock shop (as Claudine's omnivorous attention automatically noted and catalogued and forgot), cigars. Claudine

16

thrust people aside, murmuring, "Sorry, folks—the law, you know." She and the king stood gazing down at the fetally positioned little brown-turbaned gold body—he could have been one of the Ligerian mountebanks.

The king looked at her. She showed him her handbag —perforated by a slender mangaloid knife with an eight-inch blade. "Perhaps," she suggested, "Galactic assigned me to you only in order to have an official witness to your assassination."

One of Claudine's yeomen, followed by two ship's men, presented himself, saluting. "Get him to sick bay," she directed. "Tell the doctor it was a stun-level charge, recovery in about an hour, shock treatment recommended but not required. When the suspect comes out of it, jail him. Tell Chief Tuli to report this to Captain Schwarz—it was an attack on His Majesty here. I'll question the suspect before dinner. Okay?"

"Okay," said the yeoman. "Clear the way, folks—it's all over." People rubbernecked while the body was removed—then turned to gawk at the king.

He was gone, with Claudine.

They could have been found near the rear of the watch-and-clock shop, contentedly inspecting the dusty clutter of timepieces. Some of the antiques were so old they ticked.

"Whatever you want," said the king, "ask."

"With a right good will," she assured him, "because you'll be paying me for services already rendered—not for some impossible futurity."

"You keep harping on that. Are you reopening the door?"

She looked up at him, level-browed, faintly smiling. "I am playing. No more than that, my liege."

"Admit that you're flirting."

"Admit that it's pleasant."

"It can also be frustrating."

She went sober. "Then let's change the subject. I honestly like you, but—no dice."

"The original subject was—what can I buy you?"

17

"I want," she announced, "a wristwatch."

"What's that?"

"Very expensive. Very old."

"The first part is fine, the second is probable—but what *is* a wristwatch?"

"A sort of primitive cutichron that you strapped on your wrist."

"Sounds cumbersome," he commented, glancing at the tiny platinum cutichron on his left small fingernail.

"Find the shopkeeper," she commanded, "and ask to see some. You'll be charmed!"

Looking imperiously around over customer heads, the tall king spied a black-haired golden man hunched behind a waist-high counter at the back of the shop, inspecting something: a jeweler's glass was screwed into his eye. Drawing Claudine toward him, the king cleared his throat. The man looked up, mouth open a little, expertly letting the eyeglass drop into his palm.

"We would like to see—" began the king, ". . . *what?*" he backhanded at Claudine.

"Wristwatches," she helped.

The man's mouth stayed open somewhat, he looked like a young-old, wise, weazened kewpie; his black hair was parted in the center and slicked back, revealing a narrow forehead with fine wrinkles; the eyebrows were expressive pencil-lines; the eyes were large and black, the nose aquiline, the face rounded-pointed, the chin surprisingly strong—and the figure, now it had straightened, surprisingly tall. The corners of the wondering mouth turned just a mite upward. "Wristwatches," he repeated in a husky voice that might once have been tenor. "Yes—I have eleven of them. But in the back—not here—" He seemed indecisive.

"We hate to intrude," Claudine suggested.

His mouth closed, he looked—not sad, but melancholy: Cyrano with less nose, brooding. "You *must* intrude: I don't dare bring them out. Just follow, please—" He arose with dignity and moved with grace to the back wall, opening inward a little door that they hadn't seen, pausing there holding it open for them. Claudine moved

18

decisively forward, the king following—he had to stoop very low.

They came erect in a dim six-by-ten workshop, the floor space no more than three by six because of littered workbenches and tray-drawer cabinets. The watchmaker puzzled over drawers.

The king whispered: "You left my back unguarded out there, Henchwoman."

She whispered back: "One knife a night is all they can afford, Wenchman."

"Ah, *here*," said the watchmaker, pulling out a drawer and laying it on a workbench, pushing aside scattered parts.

They gazed on the gleaming contents.

"They *look* like timepieces," the king ventured.

"They were worn on the wrist," explained the watchmaker, "as late as the twenty-second century. These four go back to the twentieth. The large ones are for men, the small ones for women."

Glancing again at his cutichron, the king tugged at his moustache and judged: "Monstrous."

"Beautiful!" glowed Claudine. Lifting a little gold woman's watch from the twentieth-century group, she inspected its harmonious face closely. "Jaeger-LeCoultre," she read. "How is it activated?"

The watchmaker told her: "It is activated with this little winding mechanism just under the edge-curve at the back, invisible when the watch is worn. Allow me." Gently taking the watch from her, he wound and set it by a large wall chronometer. He listened. "Musical," he declared, handing it to Claudine. She listened, and a smile of pleasure grew on her lips. She held it to the king's ear. He listened, frowning. "At night," he declared, "one would have to leave it outside one's bedroom."

"Please put it on me," she asked the watchmaker. He did so deftly, clasping the gold clasp of its black ribbon about her wrist. She admired it, secretly amused and not displeased at the discreet sliding of his fingertips along her hand as he had withdrawn them.

The king said gruffly: "How much?"

19

The watchmaker named a figure. Claudine's eyebrows went up as the king's hand dug for his billfold, and she laid a hand on his arm.

"You were going to suggest," growled the king, "that my life isn't worth that much?"

"I was going to suggest that I am on duty, and well paid. I was only teasing you, and I wanted to see the watches. Do not buy it for me."

"Would you scruple to accept flowers? For me, it is flowers. I mean this."

She squeezed his arm, smiling. It was flowers.

"How," inquired the king as he paid the watchmaker "does a Ligerian come to be dealing in Earth watches?"

Claudine's brows suddenly went level. She watched the watchmaker.

He replied blandly: "I know about the incident outside, Your Majesty. I regret that it was a Ligerian, particularly a golden Ligerian. There are three billion Ligerians, and two billion are members of my golden race. I may remark that on the continent of my origin, we do not wear turbans." He looked hesitantly at the money, shrugged, put it in a pocket. "I will give you a bill of sale." He turned to a workbench to do it.

The king and Claudine looked at each other. The king smiled faintly. Making a small mouth and a fist, Claudine gently beat her bosom.

"When you are finished with that," said the king, "please let me look closely at your watch."

2

The *Eiland of Ligeria* was a mighty catamaran: her twin white hulls, nearly a mile long and crested by gleaming white superstructure, were studded with many banks of portholes occasionally interrupted by broad gleaming surfaces of transparent crystal. Her bows were vast panes of crystal: through them from outside, a curious deep-space-nixie might dimly descry many decks, and passengers moving.

But catamaran design, which is for waterships, has its problems for spaceliners: where do you put the engines, the inertial shield, the differential mass, the repulsors—in which, that is, of the twin hulls? The benign architect of the *Eiland of Ligeria* had solved all these problems neatly; he had fused the hulls astern, lofting the stern high enough so that it did not retard waterborne surface motion, flattening it enough so that it served as a submarine stabilizer, bellying it enough to house the engines and the DM (or differential mass) and the activators of the inertial shield, tapering it astern for the best repulsor action to provide swift space-drive. No shape-peculiarity has any significance whatsoever for a vessel in space: thrust for thrust, a windmill will go as fast as a teardrop.

As for the brig, which was Claudine's target at the moment, it was astern in one of the hulls, just forward of the fusion; and on C-deck, which at that point astern was deep bottom. You couldn't get any farther astern without running into the engine room.

Just forward of the brig, the king and Claudine were joined by short chunky Lieutenant Brh, third officer (thirtyish, his skin color a clear cerise) and by a middling-tall commander with blond crew-cut hair. (Headgear, as Claudine was learning, was optional among the *Eiland*'s officers except on ceremonial occasions.) These two officers were stalked by a frosty female fencerail named Chief U. Tuli, Claudine's right-hand woman.

Brh made ceremonious presentations: "Your Majesty, this is Commander Swainson, First Officer. Commander Swainson, this is Lieutenant Claudine St. Cyr of the Galactic Police, she commands Chief Tuli here."

Making a swift command decision, Swainson first soft-saluted the king, bowing, and accepted the king's proffered hand. "A great pleasure, Your Majesty." Turning

21

then to Claudine, he extended his own hand and said: *"Enchanté."* Taking his hand warmly, she replied with solemnity: *"Mercredi." "Pardon?"* ventured Swainson.

Chief Tuli got it back on its horse by volunteering primly: "As you requested, Lieutenant St. Cyr, I informed Lieutenant Brh about the assassination attempt. However, I could not immediately inform Captain Schwarz, who is not available. I therefore informed Commander Swainson, on the advice of Lieutenant Brh."

Swainson said formally: "Naturally the captain is often unavailable, he has his own concerns. He always responds immediately when called on the crew intercom, but I felt it unnecessary to interrupt him, the matter being under control—"

"Of course," Claudine smiled, while the king brooded. "He can be informed later. Meanwhile you two can witness my interrogation of the suspect."

In Claudine's hintermind, the image of Captain Schwarz was urbanely smiling. She'd met him at takeoff: he'd been gallant, too. He was late-thirtyish maybe (but he *could* be mid-fortyish), blond (slight curl in hair), square-jawed (slight dimple in chin), blue-eyed, very wide mouth easily smiling. *He'd* been the handsomest man she had ever seen, until the Great Doré. Well, so captains need solitude; at least, he kept in touch. . . .

Swainson led the way into the brig, stooping slightly at the door; the king followed, stooping even more; even Claudine had to stoop a little, and so of course did Chief Tuli. There was a twelve-by-eight anteroom with a yeoman on duty, and, in the depths, three barred cells; two empty, one containing the little brown-turbaned golden Ligerian. He glared at them through bars.

Swainson turned to Claudine. "Out here—or in there —or through the door?"

"In there," she elected.

The yeoman keyed the doorlock with his coded magnet. Claudine entered, and the door slid shut behind her. The three men and Tuli watched and listened.

Claudine stood before the Ligerian who had sunk down on the bed, cowering a little, watching her closely.

Her feet were slightly apart, her hands clasped behind her back, "Why?" she asked in the galactic trader-pidgin. He sat open-mouthed, stolid, scared.

Claudine then performed a curious gesture: placing the four fingers of her left hand together pointing downward, she parted the first two fingers from the last two, forming an inverted V-cleavage; and bringing up her straight right hand, she smartly cleft this cleavage. *"Why?"* she repeated.

The Ligerian eyes bugged out, and he released a flow of pidgin. The yeoman had a recorder going.

Seven minutes later, the Ligerian stopped talking and shriveled into himself. Claudine had not interrupted. A full minute longer she stood inspecting him, feet apart, hands clasped behind. She nodded once. He collapsed on the bunk, sobbing. She turned and signaled the yeoman, who let her out.

In the anteroom, she stood for a moment in thought. The others watched her, not asking questions, waiting. She jerked her head toward the outer door. The five of them left the anteroom, and the door closed behind them.

Here in the narrow corridor she turned on the king. "Did you catch the gist of that, Your Majesty?"

"No. I never learned pidgin."

"I thought you told me," she said softly, "that you were the most beloved ruler in the galaxy."

The back of his left hand slowly stroked his beard. "Until that knife went through your handbag, I thought I was."

"About a billion golden Ligerians hate your guts. And quite a few million of them are organized. In several hundred king-hostile organizations."

The king shrugged. "I wasn't counting that. As long as there is more than one organization, I feel dynastically secure. Especially if no whites are involved. He didn't say anything about whites, did he?"

"No. But he's obviously a minor tool, a crackpot *hash-ishim;* probably he wouldn't know."

Brh put in: "Who are his people here on the ship? We'd better root them out."

"You don't know pidgin either, Lieutenant?"

23

Brh cracked a crooked grin. "I don't trade."

"My, my," she murmured, "how nicely the lieutenant turns a compliment! Well; but it seems our assassin is quite alone on this ship, in terms of plotters, and I tend to believe him; he *is* one of the mountebanks, but the others didn't know he had a mission; seems word got abroad in Ligeria that the king would be returning on this voyage, so this little fellow shipped on at the suggestion of his cronies at home base." She turned to stern Commander Swainson: "More than half your crew are Ligerians, and a large number of them are golden. Do you think a shakedown is indicated?"

Swainson frowned. "I'll discuss it with the captain, but I'm not ready to recommend—" He paused, gazing over Claudine's head, beyond her.

Claudine turned. Impassively facing her was a short slender dour golden Ligerian. He was scarcely taller than she. He wore the stripes of a commander.

Swainson said: "Your Majesty, this is Commander Suren, the engineering officer. Commander, these ladies are Lieutenant St. Cyr and Chief Tuli of the Galactic Police." Silent nods were exchanged, and Suren immediately looked back at Swainson.

"Go ahead," said the first officer.

The engineer said: "Commander, you must come with me immediately. Bring these people if you wish—we may need a police officer."

Without waiting for a reply, he turned and led the way to the engine room.

Claudine had no comprehension at all of the complex repulsor engines and associated mechanisms and computers that animated the aftersection of the *Eiland of Ligeria*. All distinction among decks disappeared here: there was only one gigantic space, tapering conically astern, threaded with perforated metal catwalks and bristling with electronic machinery. The Ligerian engineer Suren led the way rapidly along a catwalk, down a companionway, along another catwalk, around a noise-pumping curve, down another companionway, along another catwalk—and stopped dead. "Look," he commanded, pointing downward.

All of them leaned on the rail, peering down through slanted windows of plate crystal into the ship's hell. The illumination was blue; and most of the catacomb was occupied by a gigantic high-polished semitranslucent sphere whose hue was—well, presumably in daylight it would be rubine red, although just here the blue lighting seemed to be conferring a purplish tinge upon its iridescence. The upper surface of the great ball was just below the level of their feet; its lower surface was lost in the depths. It seemed to have no support; actually it floated in freefall.

Claudine, between the engineer and the first officer, glanced up at Swainson. He was frowning. He said slowly: "It looks too purple."

"Exactly," Suren responded.

"Can you change the lighting?"

Suren touched a button, and the light went red. Nevertheless the sphere stayed purplish, although a trifle less so.

"Funny," Swainson commented. "Any ideas, Suren?"

"None."

"Ever see it like this before?"

"No."

"It's a new one, though. Is it maybe different?"

"As you know, we took it on in New York."

"Extravagant, too—on *this* voyage, of all voyages!"

"Had to," Suren reminded him.

"True. Anyhow—is it maybe different by nature?"

"Same model. No new ingredients."

"How did it look when we first mounted it?"

"Normal."

"So when did you notice this coloring?"

Pause. "Soon after we reached trans-light velocity."

Claudine cleared her throat. "Excuse me, but Commander Suren mentioned that he might need a police officer—so may I take a moment to dig this, a little?"

"Go ahead," said Swainson. Suren glowered at the sphere.

"First of all—what is it?"

25

Swainson passed it. "Suren?"

The small yellow-skinned engineer moistened thin pink lips with a pointed pink tongue and said: "The DM-component."

After a moment, Claudine tried: "Stretch that out a little."

"You don't even know what that means?"

"Component, yes. DM, no."

Suren tongued lips again. Staring at the sphere, he tried to put engineering physics into one-syllable words—and he failed, but at least he minimized syllables.

"Starships have to go faster than light. Supposedly nothing *can* go faster than light. But we cheat with the DM—that stands for Differential Mass. The faster we go, the more massive that sphere gets. By the time we hit the speed of light, the mass that we feel *here* is greater than the combined mass of all the stars as we feel it here. So we keep going faster and faster."

Claudine pondered. Claudine said: "Why?"

"Look, miss, we don't have all day. Just believe it."

Claudine swallowed and said: "All right. Maybe that's all I *need* to know about the DM. Now tell me why you thought you might need a police officer."

Lip-tonguing. Then: "If anything is wrong with the DM, maybe somebody tampered with it."

Visions of Promethean dwarfs pilfering fire from the sun! Claudine snapped: "Now how could anybody tamper with a thing like that?"

"I don't see how anybody could."

"So?"

"So you're the police officer."

Grinning suddenly, Claudine murmured: "Is there a doctor in the house?" Sobering quickly, she asked the next question: "If that thing breaks down, what happens?"

Brh closed his eyes and said, "Oh, my, God!"

Swainson snapped: "Lieutenant!"

Gently the king put in: "Claudine—we are now moving at trans-light velocity. If the DM should break down—all of us would simply cease to exist."

26

Claudine pondered the cataclysmic prospect. She turned to Swainson: "Then why don't we play it safe and cut down below the speed of light?"

"To cut out the DM, we would have to cut down *way* below the speed of light. It would take us twenty-five or thirty years to reach Ligeria."

"I see. Then why don't we return to Earth and make another try later?"

"That would not be an easy decision. We are already more than a light-year away from Earth."

"In seven hours? And that's how many trillion miles?"

"Quite a few," said Swainson. "So even to go home—below light speed, it might take us nearly a year to get there."

Suren volunteered: "Commander Swainson wants first to be sure that something is really wrong."

"It's pertinent," Brh inserted, "that on half-rations, our food supply would last just about six months. We're weak on hydroponics."

"Cute," observed Claudine. She thought. She turned to Suren: "May I go down?"

Nodding once, he led the way far astern to a crystal hatch below which she could see a vertical ladder. He paused here to open a locker. "You'll need protective suits. Too much oxygen in there, and some other mean stuff. Anybody else going?"

All of them affirmed. Suren passed out suits that looked like clear plastic rainsuits with globular helmets.

"Another thing," Suren cautioned. "There's no artificial gravity in there, the DM-sphere is very massive and has to float gravity-free. It is held in position by six reverse-gravity pusher-beams. But the catwalks have local artificial gravity. Stay on them, or you'll freefall."

He opened the crystal hatch, exposing the ladder-head. Down this ladder he nimbled. Swainson and Brh found themselves flanking Claudine who stood at the ladder-head. Brh said: "May I—" But he said it to a down-ward-disappearing head of dark female hair. And an instant later they were bypassed by Chief Tuli, and then by the king.

27

Brh inquired: "Commander, with the ladies gone, may I say, what the hell?"

"What the hell," said Swainson, going over. Brh followed.

Dropping off the ladder's foot, Claudine found herself on a narrow metal catwalk that sloped down forward. "Follow me," said the waiting Suren, and he started downward. She followed; and presently she found herself looking *up* at the mighty sphere, instead of down. It was just as big and just as purple—and sure enough, it *did* float free of the hull floor.

"Can I go under it?" she inquired through her helmet intercom.

"Prowl all you want," Suren snarled, "but remember you're in freefall as soon as you leave the catwalk. Use those handholds in the floor. Your headgear will protect you from the atmospheric mishmash—but don't touch the sphere, or you may become part of it. And don't stick your hand into that latticework right under it—if you do, the antigrav will snap your hand off."

Stooping, Claudine worked her way clear under the bottom of the sphere, marveling at her abrupt loss of weight: her feet floated. The DM hung four feet from the floor; she felt like Aladdin in the poison-wall cave-corridor. Glancing at the metallic lattice that she was supposed to avoid, she saw something. Moving quickly around to screen her action from the others, she managed to get a thin-gloved fingernail under an edge of the thing she'd spotted on the lattice and peel it off rather easily and slip it into a work pocket. Just for the look of it, she felt around a bit longer. Then, sighing, she came out from under, straightened, and massaged the small of her back.

"Find anything?" asked Suren.

"Just smoothery," she responded. "Tell me, Commander—if this DM *was* fooled with, when could it have happened?"

He snapped: "Before 1202 hours."

"Why?"

"That was when we hit light-velocity. It would have to

have been before that. In fact, it would have to have been long before that."

"All right. Before that—was the engine room covered?"

"I've been here myself since before takeoff. I have been accompanied by eight to twenty crewmen. Even during shore turnaround, there are always several men on watch."

The king whispered to Claudine: "What time is it now?"

She glanced at her cutichron, visible through the glove. "1747 hours."

"I am offended that you did not consult the Jaeger-LeCoultre."

Claudine looked at him. Then, really for the first time since they had left Frolic Street, she looked at the ancient watch on her left wrist. Her left eyebrow twitched a little. Dropping her hands, inconspicuously covering the watch with her right hand as she did so, she grinned and told him: "It's keeping time pretty well, Your Majesty. I'd forgotten about it—forgive me."

He smiled: "Understandable, my dear." He went sober, watching Swainson and Suren.

Inconspicuously Chief Tuli moved in, murmuring to Claudine: "Anything I should be doing?"

"Yes. Get us gracefully out of here."

Tuli cleared her throat, and her hard voice announced: "Excuse me, gentlemen, but I am growing faint. May we go upstairs now?"

Claudine's mouth dropped open. So did the king's. The others merely looked at her, and Suren queried: "Do you have all you need, Miss St. Cyr?"

"All for now," she said. "No evidence of anything. Please keep me posted on developments down here. Mind if I send in a couple of yeomen to fingerprint the bottom of this thing?"

In her room—having locked the door to the corridor, and trusting the king's promise that he would not barge through their intercommunicating door—she got out the

29

bit of paper that she had peeled off the bottom of the DM-component.

The paper was a long narrow band with rounded corners—almost four centimeters long by half a centimeter wide. It was plain on the underside where the stickery was; but on the show-side it was printed with high-gloss ink: background white, all-around border gold, lettering gold. The lettering said:

SODIM E GOMORRH

It was somehow familiar. She said it over a few times aloud. Abruptly it came to her:

SODOM AND GOMORRAH!

Wrong association, doubtless—it was a foreign tongue, Ligerian maybe; on the other hand, the Ligerians, the white ones, did have the Judaic-Christian Bible, and missions were taking it into the golden countries.

Was it a warning—or, dismal thought, simply a *forecast*—planted on the DM-component by one who had tampered with it so that in mid-career the ship would suffer the fate of the Sinful Cities of the Plain?

Absently holding the bit of paper before her lips, gently she blew upon it, meditating. Wouldn't you think that Engineering Officer Suren would have discovered it himself in the course of routine inspection?

3

Diurnal time has little meaning in deep space: their gaslit-starlit frolic had been a matinée; but now it was "really" evening, if dinnertime signals that. The king should by protocol have sat at the captain's right, with Chief Tuli standing behind the king for security while Claudine languished at another table; but just before dinner, Captain Schwarz and the king had shaken hands, and both had looked at Claudine (dark skin, white satin gown, low décolletage, no jewelry except slender synthetic diamond ear-pendants), and both had told each other in a commingling breath: "Protocol be damned!" whereupon the king and the captain had joined in a merry placecard-moving (which terminated in the displacement of an end ensign to the floor), and a large new placecard labeled CLAUDINE was fabricated by the captain out of a menu and placed between captain and king.

The captain's table was the chamber-of-commerce-speakers'-table type: maybe a hundred feet long, and dignitary-loaded, raised on a half-meter dais at one end of the enormous first-class dining salon just forward of amidships in the superstructure above the twin hulls. It was a period salon, Post-Medieval Twentieth Century, with a single exception: instead of spreading cubistic chandeliers overhead, there were only real stars.

Claudine estimated more than three hundred diners—all dressed formally—the men much like twentieth-century white-tie bon vivants (except with short jackets and cummerbunds instead of tails), the women like Late Minoan Parisiennes (flounced skirts, and bosoms that would have been bare were it not for diaphanous sheathings). All tables except the captain's table were circular, damask-covered, sterling-serviced, each seating eight diners and large enough for twelve. The music was a real thirty-seven-piece string ensemble (no electronic instruments) at the far end of the salon on another dais: you could hear it as loudly or as softly as the consensus at your round table might wish, through an audio outlet at each table controllable by the man designated table chairman.

The captain, however, had a special option on the audio. In the middle of the brandied grapefruit the handsome blond arose, flicked off the string ensemble, flicked on the master control, and said blandly in a melodious tenor: "Sorry to interrupt your pleasure, friends, but there is a little matter of an exvocation—"

They quieted: *exvocation*? Fascinated Claudine could nevertheless not restrain her professional vision from sweeping the salon during this lull. Just in front of the captain's table, three tables were chaired by the ship's top officers: from left to right, by Commander Suren, by First Officer Commander Swainson, and by Second Officer Lieutenant-Commander Mashti. (Lieutenant Brh was away on duty.) Farther back in the salon, could she pick out any known faces? eh, at a table not far away sat that delectable golden Ligerian transpositor, the Great Doré, but he seemed to be the only one she knew. No mountebanks, naturally. Was that the dowager halfway back? Claudine had seen her only in a compact mirror. On a hunch, she looked for the watchmaker, but couldn't find him. . . . Well, but naturally not: he wasn't first-class, like the star Doré. . . .

"We are gathered," orated Captain Schwarz, the corners of his wide mouth turned upward a bit, "for the final voyage of the *Eiland of Ligeria*—the mightiest spaceliner ever built. I am sure that all of you have been briefed on this retirement voyage, but here are the salient features. We are traveling at a leisurely cruise pace from Earth, which is Sol IV, to Ligeria, which is Altair VII. We will traverse this distance of seventeen light-years in approximately six days, although our normal commercial run has been four; but our mood is to be one of leisurely gaiety —let us not hasten the end. Any of you can calculate in your head that our average speed will be in the neighborhood of 1035 C—that is, one thousand and thirty-five times the velocity of light. Our peak velocity, just before we go into mid-trip freefall, will be double that, or about 2100 C; this peak velocity will be attained day after tomorrow, early in the afternoon."

They were listening attentively, and they shared his mood-change when *weltschmerz* crept subtly into his voice:

"Our beloved *Eiland* has sailed the star islands of our

galaxy for a score of years. My revered predecessor, Captain Vlodni, was her first captain, and I am her second: I have served aboard her for a decade, two years as second and first officer to Captain Vlodni, eight years in command. I wish I could say that the *Eiland* was about to be retired in graceful yielding to a still greater ship. Unhappily—and I say this as a conservative, and it may cashier me as a captain—she is being retired for only one reason: economy. Her successors—two of them—will be much smaller, much faster—and much cheaper."

He stopped there: his mouth-corners had drooped, he was frowning down. The salon was unhappily quiet. Claudine and the king exchanged melancholy glances.

Up went the captain's head. "I said that this will be a six-day voyage. The *Eiland* normally does it in four days. Her successors will bring it off in three days at an energy saving of thirty percent, without taking account of reduced crew and increased passenger turnover. Every pale commercialized leukocyte in my bloodstream applauds this decision; every red corpuscle of love and adventure and aesthetic appreciation deplores it. And I judge that many of you feel the same. For most of you passengers in this first-class salon have no reason whatever to travel to Ligeria at this time: you are here to do final homage to the *Eiland*. Even in the cruise-class salons, numerous passengers have changed their plans at great inconvenience to make this voyage aboard the *Eiland*; and these honored passengers also are now listening to my voice."

Now that same voice took on a saber-edge. "And what is the destiny of the incomparable *Eiland of Ligeria?* His Majesty the King of Ligeria has purchased the *Eiland* for his planet. There she will be—*reprocessed.*"

Dull silence. They knew. The king sat placid.

"She will become," said Schwarz, "a hundred thousand Ligerian ground-skimmers and an untellable number of children's toys. She will become, in a word—atomically resynthesized *scrap.*"

Slowly he turned to look at the king, who slowly turned to look at him.

The captain's voice went smooth again. "This is the

end of an era. It is my hope and prayer that in due course there will be pressure—possibly engendered by some of *you*—either to put the *Eiland* back into service, or to build a new *Eiland* even greater than she. There is no substitute for luxury—no substitute for leisure—no substitute for galactic grace among the stars."

He sat abruptly.

There was no applause.

After a long minute, one by one, tables began flipping on the musical audio. But it stayed diminuendo.

What now filled Claudine's mind was the *Eiland* pride of Captain Schwarz during their takeoff run down East River. Was that only this morning? The captain and three privileged passengers stood hard in the bow of one of the catamaran hulls, gazing through the perfect transparency of the thick crystal plating. They were on E-deck (the decks went down to H), and the bow waves plashed at their feet; and above them the sky was perfection, deep blue with bleached white cotton-puffs floating.

"From each planet and each port," Captain Schwarz told his guests, "I have a special takeoff procedure, but it always follows the same principle. Here at the Port of New York, we travel on the surface down East River past the great buildings and under the bridges—comfortably clearing Triborough Bridge III, almost scraping the post-medieval Manhattan and Brooklyn bridges—and out into Upper New York Bay: this allows the spectators from this deck upward to view the city, and to wave an ecstatic farewell to the Second Statue of Liberty, and at the same time not to be depressed by the sadness of submarine bleach in the contaminate East River. Once in New York Bay, though, we hit something like pure salt water; and at this point the ship sinks a bit, and everybody from C-deck downward is under water. Finally, debouching into Lower New York Bay, we will go airborne—"

Claudine, standing between captain and king, found her interest three-ways divided among the view and the speech and the speaker. Schwarz was gazing at onrushing baywater. Intuitively Claudine glanced up at the face of her escort: the king was, as she had guessed, watching Captain Schwarz rather than the view, and his expression was ambiguous. When the captain had welcomed the king aboard, the two men had manifested old cordial acquaintance, but there had been hostility in the psychic undertow.

She glanced backward, checking her infield. There stood Chief U. Tuli, tall, angular, brunette-prim, the hem of her herringbone skirt correctly cutting the midline of her knees.

Schwarz said low: "Watch, now." Claudine swung back to the bow crystal.

The water that waved at Claudine's feet burbled upward, rose above her head, disappeared. There was emerald green. There were scared fish. On this deck there were no lights: all was submarine-eerie.

Schwarz said low: "Quite an introduction to outer space, don't you think?"

"Quite," said the king, who had seen it twice before on two other planets.

Fish ran away from them.

And then, Claudine recalled, Schwarz had said the thing. "This is all quite unnecessary, you know," he remarked. "Our catamaran hulls are unnecessary—pure luxury, for beauty and for *this*. The *Eiland of Ligeria* is *all* pure luxury."

Silence.

Claudine said brokenly: "I am appreciating it."

Schwarz turned to her quickly. "Thank you, miss. I have a long-range affair, you know, with the *Eiland*. I wish I could be sure that her successors would be as concerned about the intricacies of sheer human experience. That is what we are *for*, I think. All the work is ultimately for that."

She answered, watching fish run away: "Let us hope people will continue to demand this for their money."

"Thank you."

Silence.

"By now," the captain informed them, "we are through the Narrows and into Lower New York Bay. We go airborne now, and we circle back over Manhattan. Again, you see, it is unnecessary. But you like it, don't you?"

"We do," affirmed the king.

"To augment your pleasure," suggested the captain, "From time to time glance above you: there is a TV screen, it is activated from the ship by a species of mirror radar: you will see the ship objectively, rising out of the water."

Claudine felt as though she were wearing bifocals with a different image in each lens. Below, peering through the crystal picture window, she watched the water lighten and surface appear and go downward and disappear below, leaving only bright sky in the window that dripped with latent water. Above, in the TV screen, she watched the ship's exterior from what appeared to be a distance of a few hundred meters—at first with only her superstructure visible above waterline, then rising until the twinness of her hulls began to appear, then rising farther until only the keels touched water—then going wholly airborne, with water dripping away from her keels, drops gleaming in sunlight.

"I consider this sublime," the king declared.

Claudine said: *"Si."*

Schwarz responded: *"Danke."*

They soared above Manhattan.

"In a moment we will spatialize," the captain mused aloud. "We will not put her nose upward, we will simply rise so that you can continue to watch below. Then, at a thousand kilometers off Earth—in about ten minutes—off we go."

Manhattan floated away behind them.

"And now," declaimed Schwarz, "the stars."

4

The Claudine mind returned to the St. Cyr body: it was in the dining salon, moving in universal silence through potage and wine and fish and wine.

The entrée was *roshif,* accompanied by Burgundy.

The king gently reft the pall. "Definitely not beef," he remarked to the captain across Claudine.

"Better?" Schwarz inquired gloomily.

"Better," affirmed the king, while Claudine nodded.

"Prime Lahkschmi," said Schwarz, cutting and inserting.

"Mm," agreed the king. *"That's* it, then. Just offhand, I'd say—Walmsley Lahkschmi, four-horned, castrate, no more than eight months old."

The captain eyed stars. "If they followed my orders," he semi-affirmed, "Walmsley Lahkschmi, four-horned, castrate, seven months."

The king sipped Burgundy.

Claudine, about to help the chat along, was diverted by a slight disturbance near the back of the salon—portside (to her right) where stars shone through generous windows. There was a door back there, and several waiters and an officer were clustered around some unruly somebody or something: the people at the nearest tables were twisted around, staring.

Chief Tuli, standing behind the king, leaned over and whispered to Claudine: "It's old Fire-Eyes."

"Greco?"

"Greco."

"I didn't know he was aboard. Why isn't he making any noise?"

"Maybe somebody has hold of his mouth—"

Whoever it was let go. A horning high baritone filled the salon without benefit of audio: "Hearken ye potbellied denizens of Sodom and Gomorrah! Ye shall die in the Holy Fire—"

Sodim e Gomorrh! Him?

The cluster of waiters and officers swayed and struggled like a whole football team trying to quell an unruly fullback; those at the nearest tables were on their feet, alarmed, among them Suren, Swainson, Mashti, and (farther back, nearer to the disturbance) Doré; the captain arose, so did the king, so did Claudine, so did all at the captain's table; others began to stand, but Captain Schwarz claimed the audio control and commanded: "This is the captain! All passengers seated! All passengers seated!" The king sat; so did Claudine; so gradually did the others, alternately looking at the disturbance and at the captain.

Old Fire-Eyes burst out of the huddle, ran front and center, and took a stance fifty feet from the captain where he could command the salon. He was almost seven feet tall, clad in rags, his arms and chest tattered-bare, face gaunt, untidy white patriarch-beard, eyes enormous. Pointing a stringy arm and finger straight at the captain, he opened wide his jaws and horned: "The *Eiland of Ligeria* is the ultimate symbol of human corruption! She shall die among the stars, and all aboard shall die—"

They muffled him and hauled him away.

Tense quiet.

Mouth-corners up again, the captain said quietly on the audio so all could hear: "Walmsley Lahkschmi, fourhorned, castrate, seven months." A ripple of laughter rewarded him as he resumed his seat and went to work on this patrician *rosbif*.

Claudine leaned toward the king. "If the captain doesn't already know about the knife-throwing and the purple DM-component, shouldn't we—"

"Not yet," the king suggested. "Wait for dessert."

She nodded and ate.

38

Presently the captain turned to her. "I must apologize, Lieutenant, for being preoccupied."

"You have reason, Captain."

Their eyes met, and lingered in the meeting. His momentarily flickered downward, then up to hers again: so gracefully swift had he appreciated her décolletage. Up came her mouth-corners—and up came his.

He said: "Your eyes are quick."

She said: "Yours do not have to be furtive."

His held hers a moment longer—then his deliberately lowered. While he inspected her beauty, she watched his forehead: it was a *good* forehead.

His eyes came back to hers. *"Magnifique!"* he told her.

"You sound as though I were a little like the Statue of Liberty."

"I had Ariadne more in mind."

"You are graceful."

"Please make that *gracious*. It is you who are graceful."

The king ate Lahkschmi.

Holding her eyes, the captain challenged: "After dinner, I suggest a solitary discussion of your grace."

Holding his eyes, she countered: "Sir, I am not a Minoan princess; it is more of a mongrel cop that I am."

"For that matter, I am not a Minoan prince; it is more of a Nordic space-dog that I am. What does that do for or against us?"

This fencing was close! Said Claudine with an impudent grin: "Nordic-Schmordic. After dinner, I suggest a solitary discussion of police matters. The king was nearly assassinated this afternoon."

The king choked over his last sip of Burgundy. Waiters appeared, switching courses.

Now the captain's blue eyes were luminous, he was smiling openly. "You flirt well," he told her, "and you keep your distance without offense. Definitely, Lieutenant —a solitary police discussion: pray accept my arm after dessert."

"With all my heart. There is also a little matter about a DM-component."

39

"I know. But in your absence with me—what will you do about the king? Not that I want to say anything to prevent—"

"He will be covered."

The king sighed. Tuli stiffened.

The captain added: "And after the police matters are done?"

"It is you who are the captain."

"It remains, however, that you are an officer."

"Doesn't it, just!"

Both of them were grinning broadly, appreciating each other wholly.

The captain's grin froze, it became a rictus, his blue eyes bugged and glazed. Stiffened so, he stared at Claudine an instant longer—and collapsed with his face in his plate.

5

Commander Swainson convened a command officers' emergency call within half an hour of the captain's death. Dessert had been served, but nobody had stayed for it; the steward, getting the picture, had them take it away. Swainson invited the king to be present as ship's owner, and Claudine and Tuli as Galactic Police people. The ship's doctor, Commander Hastings, was excused: obviously he had coroner duty.

They sat in the captain's conference room just aft of the bridge. Acting Captain Swainson, chairing it, sat reluctantly in the captain's chair at the head of the long diamond-shaped metal table. At his left sat Lieutenant-Commander Mashti, the second officer; Lieutenant Brh, the third officer; and Commander Suren, the gold-Ligerian engineering officer. The king of Ligeria brooded at Swainson's right; beside him sat Claudine and then Tuli.

Leaning heavily on the table with both arms, Acting Captain Swainson eyed them all one by one and stated: "I guess I don't just know why I have called this conference. But we have to have it. You all know I'm the skipper now."

They all nodded.

Swainson rubbed his mouth on a gold-braided cuff and looked up again. Claudine noticed very small tear-beginnings in his eye-corners: she watched them while he talked—somehow they shrank and vanished. Swainson said: "He took this trip hard. That was probably it. Heart failure. Maybe it was best."

Claudine gently tugged at the king's sleeve. The king inquired: "Do we *know* that it was heart failure?"

Swainson looked at him hard. Then he replied: "Pending the autopsy by Dr. Hastings, that's the tentative verdict."

Claudine tugged again. The king suggested: "If you don't mind, sir—" He paused.

Swainson stared at him. Then he slowly looked around at the other officers: they all sat stolid. Swainson turned back to the king. "As I said, Your Majesty, I really don't know why this conference, except as a formality. We all know what to do now: Commander Mashti has become first officer, Lieutenant Brh second officer; I will appoint an acting third officer, and we will carry on. However, if you have anything—"

The king observed: "It might be worthwhile to have a word from Lieutenant St. Cyr, since you have seen fit to invite her here."

Swainson stared at Claudine and nodded once.

Claudine was in her business mood: level-browed, hard-eyed, mouth narrower than usual: her revealing white evening gown rather conferred irony upon this mood. "Captain, I have several things. First, with your permission, I should like to know from Dr. Hastings when to expect the results of the autopsy."

Swainson considered. He suggested: "Perhaps Chief

Tuli will be good enough to use the phone, there, and inquire."

Claudine nodded to Tuli, who cleared her throat and arose lankily and departed for the phone.

"Next," said Claudine, "I should like to review the events of the afternoon. I note that Commander Mashti is the only one present who may not know all that you and I know. Bluntly, Captain, is there any reason why I should not speak freely before Commander Mashti?"

"None," averred Swainson, while Mashti regarded Claudine with faintly paranoid hostility. He was a medium-sized indigo bald Maruvian, toothless (they were sapsuckers).

Claudine stated: "When these untoward events are teased out of the trivia and laid side by side, their togetherness troubles me. First, a golden Ligerian threw a knife at the king. Next, Commander Suren discovered an unusual purplish coloring in the DM-component—on whose well-being the life of the ship depends. Third, during dinner, Fire-Eyes Greco created a disturbance and threatened the death of the ship. Soon afterward, Captain Schwarz dropped dead."

They all brooded heavily.

Swainson said low: "Do you see any connections?"

"Not yet," said Claudine. "But in all candor I must point out that I was the one nearest the king when the knife was thrown, and also the one nearest the captain when he dropped dead."

Swainson gazed at her moodily. The king sat expressionless. Swainson said: "Your identification, Lieutenant."

Claudine reached in her handbag and drew out an ID card. Swainson accepted it, arose, took it to a computer, and fed it in; meanwhile Claudine arose, sat before the computer, and placed her forehead between electrodes. A light glowed green, and the card came out. Swainson restored it to Claudine, and both resumed their seats; Tuli had returned and was seated.

The king remarked: "She stopped the knife with her handbag."

Swainson asserted in a speculation-terminating tone: "She is not a suspect, she is a Galactic Police officer." He turned to Tuli: "What did you learn, Chief?"

"Sir, Dr. Hastings says that he feels the autopsy must be completed before he can venture an opinion. He will not have a report before 1000 hours tomorrow."

It chilled all of them a little.

Swainson turned to Suren. "Commander—any recent developments with the DM-component?"

Suren had his hands flat on the table, fingers spread; he consulted these hands as he said: "Immediately upon the captain's death, when the salon began to clear, I took occasion to go aft. The purple hue has deepened slightly, but there is another thing. This is vague, but I will try to say it. I think now that the purple has become more of a maroon, and it is restricted to a sort of gross core that occupies the central two thirds of the sphere; the outside of the sphere appears to have resumed its normal rubine red. Without question, Captain, the phenomenon is developing."

Unshaken, Swainson inquired: "Any theory?"

"None yet."

Swainson looked about him. "Does anyone else have a theory?"

All slowly shook their heads.

"What are your plans, Commander?"

Suren, continuing to gaze at his hands, replied: "Tonight I will run some radioactivity tests."

Silence.

Swainson said evenly: "It interests me that, just at this time, Captain Schwarz should have died. He knew how to deal with a situation involving imminent failure of the DM-component."

Suren's head snapped up. "He *did?*"

"Don't *you?*" responded Swainson, surprised.

Suren colored—the blush was greenish. "I didn't think there *was* a way."

"Well, there is," said Swainson, "and as ship's engineer, you ought to be acquainted with it. Why aren't you?"

Swallowing, Suren mumbled: "I won't lie. They lectured about it in the final training course for my master engineer's papers. It seemed like a pretty way-out impossibility. I don't go for way-out stuff. I guess I didn't listen much. Anyhow, I forgot."

Swainson went cold. "Your honesty is noted," he finally snapped. "I will retrain you. However, it will take several hours, and the necessity does not seem immediate. Can you meet with me at 1100 hours tomorrow—after I have the autopsy report from Dr. Hastings?"

"Certainly. Where?"

"I'll come to your office."

"Aye aye, sir."

Lull . . .

Commander Mashti suggested, lisping slightly: "Thir, out of rethpect to Captain Thwartth, do you sink we thould pothtpone or canthel the thoot tomorrow morning?"

Swainson stiffened: he respected Mashti as a competent officer, but the lisp affected him like chamois rubbed against teeth. Less courteously than he might have done, he returned: "Out of the question, Commander. I would expect you to know that Captain Schwarz would want the shoot to go on—and every other festivity planned for this voyage, to do joyous honor to the *Eiland of Ligeria.*"

Mashti shriveled a little. Glancing at the king, Claudine found that he was glancing at her. She glanced at Tuli: the chief was a glacier.

Swainson demanded with truculence: "Anything else, gentlemen? ladies?"

They shook their heads.

He stood: "Formation—dismissed."

In Claudine's room, with the door to the king's suite closed (but unlocked), she and Tuli brooded.

Tuli said: "I have an irrelevancy."

"Name it."

"It has always seemed to me a hell of a way to spell island."

Groping her way out of other considerations, Claudine

44

confronted the remark, mentally repeated it several times, got the sense of it, agreed that it seemed irrelevant, wondered how irrelevant it really was. Tuli had a way of projecting weirdities that turned out to be hits. Claudine explained: "It's a bilingual homonym."

"Thank you, Lieutenant. What's that?"

"Something we have to watch out for, all the time. A word in one language that happens to sound the same as a word in another language but means something entirely different. *Eiland* with *ei* is Ligerian for empress."

"Oh? Is there one?"

"One what?"

"Is there an empress of Ligeria, actually?"

"Concerning that," Claudine remembered, "I have questioned the king."

"And?"

"No."

"Anyhow," Tuli noted, "this ship is a kind of island in space. So maybe it's all right either way you think of it."

Part Two

THE GUNNERY-AERIE

6

The shooting gallery was vast, it might have been out-
doors: amidships, its crystal dome shone with glaring
stars in black sky, yet paradoxically its broad green mea-
dowlawn was vitalized with sunlight. The people were
dressed in sunny clothes for the shoot: the men wore
open-collar varicolored shirts, the women wore floppy
hats. It was the new gallery's premiere, open only to first-
class passengers and officers and certain invited civilian
employees of Frolic Street: if there were fewer than three
hundred present, Claudine could not tell the difference—
and yet there was no crowding.

Shooting had not begun: the acting captain was late.
Claudine and the king had plenty of time to inspect the
spacious installation. They didn't talk much, contenting
themselves with pointing out to each other the several
features: when one pointed, the other got it.

Claudine was not failing to look for people. When she
recognized someone, mentally she catalogued his presence. There was no particular order about where anybody
was; but one by one, scatteredly, she picked out Suren,
Mashti, Brh, the weazened watchmaker (whose presence
caused her to glance again at her watch and again to
shudder and cover it with her hand), the dowager, and
a number of other people who were notables of Earth and
of other planets. This peoplewatching, though, kept being
interrupted by the cap-sleeve-picking and pointing of the
fascinated king.

The feature that most engaged them was the free-float-

49

ing Gunnery-Aerie. From where they stood, at the stern side of the gallery, the Gunnery-Aerie hovered to their right, and amazingly above them: amazingly, because there was nothing visible to support it. The Gunnery-Aerie was where shooters fired from. It was a rectangular blockhouse, perhaps nine meters deep and three meters high and sixty meters long, floating in midair twenty meters above the grass: no supports at all. From its gunports projected the wicked muzzles of forty rifles. Comprehending their trajectories, the heads of Claudine and the king swung slowly left: the pits were two hundred meters from the aerial guns, with bull's-eye targets that rose and fell, revealing hits by means of white-spreading electronic spots, while a great forty-unit scoreboard centered overhead told everybody who was doing how well. . . .

The whole room—if "room" was what you should call this mighty space—was four hundred meters in either direction.

Unexpectedly Acting Captain Swainson was vocally present—confirming these estimates in a booming voice that, amplified, originated from the Gunnery-Aerie, although his body stood on the grass below it.

"Ladies and gentlemen: if we were now to take time to bow our heads to honor the memory of Captain Schwarz, the captain would be enormously irritated. He wanted this voyage to be memorable fun, and so it shall be. In the spirit of gaiety, I am honored to take his place as I present to you the most remarkable sports development of our time—the floating Gunnery-Aerie, his invention. It was installed aboard the *Eiland of Ligeria* just for this final voyage: it is the only one of its kind anywhere in the universe.

"This floating Gunnery-Aerie is supported by antigrav units. The rifles in it are entirely free in their motion up and down, left and right—they can even pepper bullets against the crystal dome, without, I assure you, damaging the dome. However, their freedom of motion *downward* is restricted: they can shoot no lower than one meter below the bottom edge of an erected target; and this means, no lower than two and one-half meters above the grass at the railing in front of the target pit. Surely all of you can see the meaning for you spectators; but at the risk of being egregious, I will make the meaning specific. You can stroll at will the whole length and breadth of the gallery, all the way up to the pit, while the shooting is going on: the bullets will sail safely over your heads; no matter where you stand, no bullet can come anywhere near you."

He paused to allow the crowd to *oh* and *ah*. It did.

Acting Captain Swainson then said: "If all of you will now form yourselves in single file and pass the chief over there, he will give each of you a numbered ticket. At the conclusion of this monkey business, we will read forty winning numbers: these will be the people privileged to enter into the first shoot. About thirty minutes later, we will read forty more numbers—"

They filed past the chief. It took half an hour. Then Swainson boringly read winning numbers that were thrillingly heard. Claudine's number came up. So did the king's. For them, the drawing was rigged.

The happy, happy pair fell into line with the other joyous thirty-eight. Just below the Gunnery-Aerie, they stepped into an invisible antigrav-shaft, marked only by a white circle on the grass and a hole in the aerie floor directly above it; and after an airborne instant, they stood inside. The light was dim here, artificially red as in a photographic darkroom; no outside light filtered in around the gunports which were hermetically sealed; the gunsights were electronic, no wall-holes were needed.

"Please take any gun-station at all," said a voice. "None of them has any special advantage, each gun has its own target. When you have taken your stations, I will explain how to use these guns, which operate on post-medieval twentieth-century principles; and then you can fire at will for half an hour, after which the next forty winning numbers will be announced—"

Claudine and the king took adjacent guns and chattered together over the mechanism, not listening at all to the lecture, figuring it out for themselves. The disadvantage of this fun procedure was that they didn't hear the signal to test for windage; and when one or two shots alerted them, they began rapid fire.

The male shape next to Claudine stopped her. "Hold it up, lady. Your pitmen are cowering in the pit."

The voice was a thrilling middle-baritone. She stopped the king's firing, then peered at the stranger through eyes that had once been accustomed to this red dimness but had now been spoiled by the daylight in the gunsights. Then she recognized him. "You're the Great Doré!"

"Thank you. But I don't think we've—"

"Claudine St. Cyr. And this is His Majesty King Zhavàr of Ligeria."

"Your Majesty."

"Mr. Doré."

Claudine queried: "What are we doing wrong?"

"You aren't supposed to fire seriously yet. You have to test your pieces and adjust windage."

"What's windage?"

"Wind blowing across range makes the bullets drift. You fire a test shot, aiming at the bull's-eye. The pitman marks it with an electronic spot to show where your bullet hit the target. You notice whether it was off up, down, left, right, and how much; and you adjust this gadget on the gun to correct your aiming device, and you try again."

"That's excellent, but also silly. We're inside a ship—there isn't any wind."

"There is, however, corkscrew-rifling or grooving inside your gun. It gives torque or twist to the bullet, and the torque makes the bullet drift to the right. You have to correct for that. It's a kind of windage."

"Why don't the sights correct automatically for that?"

"In each rifle, the torque is a little different."

"This *is* primitive, isn't it!"

"Quite. However, in even earlier times, they corrected for windage without calibrated sights even."

"No!"

"Just a moment—I'll calm down your pitmen and you can try it."

He spoke into an intercom—there was one at each station—and nodded. Claudine and the king, firing carefully, spotted the mark, adjusted, fired again, spotted the new mark, adjusted, fired again, spotted the third mark, nodded to each other. "Ready to go," said Claudine.

Doré demanded: "You're sure?"

"Positive."

"You've shot before, a little?"

"A little."

"Bet?"

"Propose."

"Ten credits on ten shots."

"Is the king in?"

"Does he want to be?"

The king nodded.

Doré suggested: "Since it's three-way, two of us should prorate the winnings."

The king proposed: "Low man drops out, and the other two whack up thirty credits according to points."

"Points?" queried Claudine.

The king explained: "By convention—ten points for each bull's-eye, and the outer circles are valued eight-six-four-two. We take the total on ten rapid-fire shots."

"*Ah, bon!*" said Claudine; and Doré nodded.

"Let's fire at will," said the king.

"Wait," said Doré. "First we flag the pit—"

Thirty shots sounded like fifteen fast shots.

Pause.

Three pitmen marked the holes in the targets with ten successive markings on each target: the pitmen were enjoying this, they did it like a ballet: three—three—three. . . . At the conclusion of this reporting, the three contestants gazed at each other.

The king spoke first, counting money. "I'm out. You two get fifteen credits each. Two perfects."

"Not fair!" Doré protested. "Miss St. Cyr and I only took one hundred each—and you took a ninety-eight. That's not a clear win!"

Handing over ten credits with a flourish, the king commanded: "Take it. I was lousy."

Claudine grinned. Shrugging, Doré put all the money together, handed Claudine fifteen credits, and pocketed the rest. Then he suggested: "Want to do it again? We have another ten minutes."

"Instead," Claudine countered, "let's see if we can kill any of the spectators below."

Doré's eyebrows hit ceiling. The king drawled: "Are you out of character, Claudine—or are we learning things about you?"

"I mean it," she protested, "with qualifications. My gun is empty, I've tested. Are yours?"

To be sure, they fired at their targets and got dead clicks.

"Good," she said. "Now, according to Captain Swainson, these guns are set so they can't fire more than one meter below a target—which means that people on the grass can't possibly be hit. Let's see if it works for our guns."

"All right," agreed Doré; and the king nodded; and the three of them made earnest efforts to lower their gun muzzles. They failed.

Claudine gave up. "I guess they're safe, all right." She swung on Doré: "Mr. Transposer—can *you* shoot a spectator?"

Still working with his gun, Doré became quite still. Then he said casually: "I've had no better success than you."

"I didn't say that. I'm thinking about your stage act. Can you use your special ability to *make* your gun shoot lower?"

Releasing his gun, Doré turned to face her squarely. "As a matter of fact, I think I can."

"Then let's see you do it. I have fifteen credits that say you're bluffing."

Doré said quietly: "Sorry, but you'll have to take my word for it. There are too many sad stories about guns that weren't loaded."

Their eyes were interlocked, perfectly adapted to the dimness. . . .

The squawk-box blurted: "All shooters to ground

immediately. Something has happened." They and thirty-seven others swung around. The squawk-box coughed and corrected: "Sorry, I've had a change. All shooters stay where you are, and don't shoot. Something has happened. Out."

In a triangle, Claudine and Doré and the king exchanged concerned looks, while babble filled the Gunnery-Aerie.

Claudine snapped: "Your Majesty, tell him who I am."

The king said: "This is Lieutenant St. Cyr of the Galactic Police."

Doré said: "My compliments."

"The point is," Claudine told him swiftly, "use your special power now: sweep the ground with your gunsight and tell me what has happened."

Doré swung to his gun, and its stock elevated noticeably above prior possibility. After a moment of reconnaissance, he went motionless. Then he turned to Claudine: "Take my gun and see for yourself."

Claudine mounted Doré, seized the gun, put her eyes to the bifocal sight, and got the picture. Captain Swainson lay supine on the grass, his mouth open.

Claudine said to Doré: "Put your gun back the way it was." She dismounted.

Without a comment, Doré did so. He turned to her with a questioning expression, but he said nothing. Neither did the king.

Claudine told them warmly: "You are both good patient boys, and I thank you. Your Majesty, please don't ask Doré what he saw: you'll find out soon enough; and if he says it ever so quietly, it will be heard, and this gunnery will go up in steam. Good-bye now—I have work to do."

As she turned to go, Doré caught her arm. "I'd like to see you later."

"Good idea. Call my room." She broke away and hurried to the force-field lift: they saw her flash identification to the guard, and then she disappeared through the floor.

A few moments later Claudine was bending over the

body of Acting Captain Swainson, while a handful of officers bent over her and dozens of spectators bent over them.

Claudine stood erect and methodically eye-swept a 360-degree circuit. The ringing spectators kept her from seeing anything much beyond them, and she didn't recognize anybody.

Acting First Officer Mashti, who looked like a bald indigo Arab but whose native planet was Deneb Okab II or Maruvia, laid a slender hand on her shoulder. She turned to him: his thin face was lined, his thin lips puckered. He said uncertainly: "Dr. Hathtingth thayth he ith dead. Ith he?"

Claudine, suffering his hand, restrained an impulse and told him calmly: "Yes."

Mashti cleared his throat and observed: "He wath firtht offither. I am thecond offither."

"Then you'd better take command, since you are now in command."

"Do you—have any thuggethtionth?"

What she wanted to suggest was: "Since now you transpose *th* and *s,* why not try transposing the transpositions?" Instead she threw at him the following: "This is the last suggestion that I am going to give you—and after that, you are on your own."

"I—quite underthtand. Go on."

"Good luck," she said sympathetically, giving his shoulder a little squeeze: he would hardly have been expecting a load like this. Then she commanded flatly: "Order everybody to go to his quarters and stay there for one hour. That includes the people in the Gunnery-Aerie. Have your men enforce the order and clear this place. When it is clear, have Captain Swainson taken to the infirmary—and we go from there. Got it—*Captain* Mashti?"

He nodded. He turned to a chief and gave the order. The chief made it loudly imperative. Crewmen enforced it.

The gallery was cleared.

Mashti and another officer personally picked up Captain Swainson and carried him out.

Claudine was alone.

She stood thinking hard.

Presently she looked up at the Gunnery-Aerie.

After prolonged inspection, she was convinced. Only three gunsights had the sweep of this sector: the king's, hers, and Doré's.

True, Swainson hadn't died from a gunshot. But . . .

She hadn't done it. And the king had no reason, apart from the fact that he had no power.

But as for Doré . . .

Only—even if he *had* all unnoticed pulled some kind of transposition trick on his gun—how could that have killed Swainson?

And—most important of all—*why?*

Head down now, Claudine considered it. There was, after all, no indication that Swainson had died from anything but internal causes, possibly a heart attack. On the other hand, there was no indication that Captain Schwarz had died from anything but internal causes, possibly a heart attack. This could easily be a pyramiding of coincidence.

But if this *was* a pyramiding of coincidence, one had to include among these coincidences the Ligerian attack on the king and the alien purple in the DM-component!

Slowly Claudine shook her head. One or more of these incidents might be unrelated to any cluster—but it was entirely too probable that two or more of these incidents did inhabit some cluster. And two of them had been fatal, and one might have been fatal—and one could still be ship-fatal!

But as to the one that might be ship-fatal—the possible sabotage of the DM-component—who would have the competency or the opportunity to swing *that* one, other than the ship's engineer—a golden Ligerian?

And the man who had shot the knife at the king had been a golden Ligerian.

And the king was a white Ligerian!

Ligeria . . .

57

Frowning, Claudine in a semi-automatic gesture glanced at her cutichron—and that made her stare steadily at her new-old wristwatch—and *that* concerned her deeply.

It made her think about Doré.

Sighing deeply, she left the gallery en route to the infirmary.

She stopped dead, her guts congealed. If the ship should blow, *she* would blow with it!

Doggedly she thrust herself onward. She had been born by accident, and sooner or later she would die by accident. Forget it.

7

She found the king at the infirmary, he had the ship's senior doctor Commander Hastings involved in conversation, the king was concerned, the doctor was embarrassed. Claudine entered, taking the king's arm. "What's the problem?" she queried.

Dr. Hastings, a fiftyish Englishman, turned upon her a long, gray, smooth-shaven face: his long upper lip was prim. "Bluntly, His Majesty has asked me for my postmortem findings on the death of Captain Schwarz, and His Majesty is not the one to whom I should first be giving this information."

The king said mildly: "I didn't realize that I was embarrassing you, Doctor. Of course I will withdraw."

Claudine said crisply: "His Majesty is of course used to having his questions answered, and of course, he is ship's owner. But you were quite right, Doctor: the information should first be given to Acting Captain Mashti. But I tell you now that I need the same information, and

I hereby requisition it, and it is quite all right for His Majesty to hear it. So I suggest you now phone Commander Mashti, and inform him that we are here and what I have said, and then give him the information while we listen."

The doctor frowned. "I know that you are Lieutenant St. Cyr. Is it in your official galactic capacity that you direct me to give you the information?"

"Yes sir."

Hastings cleared his throat and looked at the ceiling. "Then I must tell you that I have not completed the diagnosis."

"Not *yet?*" the king demanded.

Claudine said gently: "Go on, Doctor."

Hastings cleared his throat and looked at the floor. "That is, I can find no direct cause of death. Indirectly, there are numerous evidences of heart stoppage."

"But the heart itself?"

"Appears undamaged. I was about to start a new procedure when His Majesty arrived."

Claudine and the king exchanged a long look. Turning back to the doctor, Claudine asked with restraint: "What effort was made to save the life of Captain Schwarz?"

Having swallowed for purposes of self-control, Dr. Hastings countered: "This is still a Galactic Police investigation?"

"Yes sir. I know that you are happy to cooperate."

"Assuredly. Captain Schwarz was dead in the dining salon. Nevertheless, on reaching the infirmary, we attempted direct endocardial electrostatic first aid; when this produced nothing, we introduced electrodes into his spinal column in the hope of restarting the heart; when the results proved negative, we opened his chest and connected the artificial heart. Nothing. Too late."

"I will not ask whether you attempted a heart transplant, which obviously would have done nothing if the artificial heart did nothing."

"Correct. We did not."

"Did you try biogesis?"

"We did; nothing. Incidentally, we have also tried all

59

these procedures on Commander Swainson without success. They are dead."

"Since we are here, I'll take occasion to view the bodies."

"Why? You saw them when they died."

"Do you appreciate having your medical procedures questioned?"

"Not particularly—"

"This is a police procedure."

"Follow me," said Hastings. He led them into his surgery—unlocking the door, and locking it behind them. A body was dimly visible through glass in an apparatus resembling an iron lung.

"Captain Schwarz," explained Hastings, "is in electronic autopsy; and since I have only the one machine, I must finish him before I can put Commander Swainson in. Commander Swainson is in the deep-freeze morgue next door. Please view the captain, and then I will take you to the commander."

Claudine, familiar with the apparatus, went to it and peered through the glass. Schwartz, covered to the chin by a sheet, was clearly visible, his blue eyes perhaps a shade glazed. She stepped back and invited the king to look: he did so with distaste, and rather surprisingly with a distinct shudder.

He turned to Claudine. "Why the sheet?"

"Modesty," she told him. "The electronics don't mind."

Hastings asked: "Will you visit Commander Swainson now? You will have to suit-up with thermal suits; I do happen to have three."

After a moment of inward debate, Claudine shook her head. "It really isn't crucial just now, and I don't want to delay your work any longer. After you have your report ready on both of them, I'll come and look at Swainson."

"Good," said Hastings candidly. He ushered them out of surgery, locking the door again, and conducted them to the corridor door.

Claudine turned to him. "Doctor, please get in touch with me as soon as you have made reasonable progress with both bodies. If necessary, start Swainson before you are satisfied about Schwarz—preferably within the hour. Tell me even any hints that you may have."

Hastings inquired slowly: "You think the deaths are connected?"

Claudine responded: "I am *guessing* that they are both heart cases—and similar. I can hardly say more than that —can I, Dr. Hastings?"

"Nevertheless," Hastings observed, "your comment has to be suggestive, Dr. St. Cyr."

The king turned a startled gaze upon her.

Claudine, darkening, tugged again at his arm, and they left.

In the corridor, strolling toward their quarters, they were silent for several paces. Presently the king made conversation. "Hastings is doing a magnificent job of maintaining a professional attitude despite what has to be a massive sorrow."

"They were his friends?"

"Schwarz particularly. They played a lot of poker."

"Who won?"

"Who do you think?"

"Well, yes."

Silent strolling.

The king stopped dead and demanded: *"Doctor* St. Cyr?"

She shrugged. "Psychology—not medicine. Forget it."

He laid a big hand on her little hand on his arm. smiled big in his big beard, and started onward, baritoning: "With your permission, my dear, this I will not forget. How about lunch in my salon?"

She raised eyebrows. "I really should grab a sandwich and get to work—"

"What could you accomplish in the next two hours?"

She frowned: "I could think."

"What kind of a psychologist are you? Don't you know that some of the best thinking is cooked on the back burner while your attention is elsewhere?"

She grinned up at him. "What's the costume? As we are?"

61

"In our shootery? Pfaugh! It will be black tie—except that I hate ties, so I will wear a white turtleneck sweater and a royal blue smoking."

"Black—tie? for *lunch?"*

"In deep space, why not?"

8

In half an hour, he quietly tried their intercommunicating door: sure enough, it was unlocked; he opened it a trifle and hesitated. She called: "I'm decent." He opened the door and stood gazing with an admiration so visible that no words were required, while Claudine assumed a mock semi-profile nose-up mannequin pose that actually was convincing. Her golden brown face, arms, and plungingly semi-revealed breasts added brilliance to her floor-flowing flame-orange gown, and there was no jewelry at all—not even ear-pendants. No, wait: she was wearing the Jaeger-LeCoultre.

He stood back in a semi-bow, offering an arm. She glided to him sidewise through the door and took the arm. He brought her a few paces into the voluptuously manly salon and pointed forward-upward. His salon was against the ship's hull; all of the far wall and much of the curved ceiling into which the curved wall flowed was a vast plate of crystal; and outside were endless flaming stars in the totality of black space.

She whispered: "You are right—it is not lunch."

The room was dim, there were candles, the table linen was damask, the service was silver, the hot stuff was in silver thermalware on a side table, the servants had come and gone. In thirty minutes he had performed this miracle? He seated her at the small centered table, stood while he poured champagne cocktails, sat opposite her while they sipped—content to study her face while beyond his shoulder she studied stars. Presently he arose to replenish the champagne and to serve both of them with chilled vichyssoise: this they leisurely spooned, it was good for Claudine's palate; she was amusedly happy to notice that he did not soil the tailored white beard that graced the top of his blue smoking. Replacing the champagne with Burgundy, he served beef Stroganoff with a side dish of haricots amandines, and they bent to this: she did not miss a fish course, it was after all really lunch, and she had always considered lettuce a nuisance. So far, no talk: just pleasure. Instead of dessert there was Roquefort-on-matzos, with Chablis.

A few moments later he paused in his nibbling to observe: "These noisy matzos have shattered our sacred silence. May I smoke? It is quieter." They were the first words that had been spoken since she had entered his salon.

"Pray do," responded Claudine, setting down her matzo. "I'm glad you drew attention to this problem of noise, because I have never seen any real reason to spoil good cheese with crackers." Scooping a tininess of Roquefort on to her knife, she lipped it and with closed eyes let it dissolve on her tongue.

As she sat savoring it, her nostrils were favored by the exquisite bouquet of the king's cigar: the bouquet of the café on Frolic Street, unique, unmistakable. After a while of Roquefort-cigar enjoyment, lazily she let her eyes open. The king, cigar pointing slightly downward out of the front of his mouth, was leaning elbows on the table, hands folded, thumbs supporting his lower lip, watching her eyes soberly. He was a damned attractive man, and the food and wines had done a delicate job of disrupting the inhibitory circuits in her forebrain. Unfortunately she knew this.

Claudine therefore said, a little tartly: "It has been delightful, Your Majesty—but I think it may be time for demitasse. A *full* cup of demitasse."

His lips curled faintly upward. "I'm in love with you," he said.

Claudine veiled her eyes, her mouth was sober, she was feeling entirely too luxurious. She murmured: "The demitasse! *Vite, Monsieur—vite!*"

"Yes, Dr. St. Cyr," he responded disconsolately, rising to pour for them both. Having poured, he took a moment to warm his hands by pressing his palms against the coffee urn. Coming then behind her, he bent over her to place the demitasse before her. As he did so, his left hand gently engaged her bare shoulder.

It was so delicious, so romantically right, that Claudine's well-wined mind had the utmost difficulty in framing coldly the problem that was central to this interpersonal warmth: how to turn him off without hurting his feelings and their working relationship, when she really didn't want to turn him off anyway.

"Why do you call me Doctor?" she temporized.

"Possibly to remind you that we are two mature people together." His fingers were not exactly tightening on her shoulder, but they were not loosening either. Claudine found that she wanted them to tighten.

"It is noontime," she reminded him.

"It is night," he insisted. Now the fingers did loosen— but only to travel a little, very delicately, just right.

Faintly she protested: "I have powdered myself with a cosmetic that is poisonous to the touch."

"Then, since it will undoubtedly kill you, I should like to die with you."

It gave her the cue. "Oh, *là,* Your Majesty," she exclaimed, seizing his searching hand with both hands, "there have been enough deaths on this ship already— and it is time for Lieutenant St. Cyr to be nosing about a bit!" Thrusting back her chair just enough to keep from hitting him with it, she leaped to her feet, swung on him with a smile, gave him the full benefit of her enchanting eyes, pressed her lips to the back of his hand, released the hand, and darted through her door, closing it.

She stood in the center of her room, back to the door, breathing heavily.

His voice came through—he was near the door. "I think you told me that you never lock it against me."

Her brows were together in acute pain. She called: "That is right, Your Majesty. And that is because we trust each other."

"Dr. St. Cyr?"

Suddenly she wheeled and ran to the door, pressing her mouth against it. "Your Majesty," she made herself say, "I want you to come through, but you must not—you must not ever. So find another woman, as I will find another man; and next time we meet, we will shake hands and laugh."

Long silence, while she died.

The king said dryly: "I like you, Claudine. So be it."

9

The telephone (no video in a bedroom) interrupted her change of clothing. She pressed the connect and answered going away. It was Lieutenant-Commander Mashti, now acting captain. "Lieutenant Tht. Thyr," he said tautly, "can you join uth for an emergenthy offitherth call at 1500 hourth?"

She glanced at her cutichron: it was a little after 1330 hours. Continuing to strip and unstrip, she replied: "Yes, Captain. Shall I bring the king?"

"No."

"Understood." .

She went back to disconnect—and then, on a thought, called Tuli. She demanded: "How are you fixed for the histories?"

"They are ready, Lieutenant."

"Please bring them here right away. I want to memorize them within the hour."

Soon she and Tuli were bending over her small sidetable, studying and exchanging an occasional word about the biographical material that Tuli had collected from the ship's files and also via some private idaradio contact with Galactic Headquarters. The following members of the crew were under consideration: the late Captain Schwarz, the late Commander Swainson, Lieutenant-Commander Mashti, Commander Suren, Lieutenant Brh, and Commander Hastings. Claudine was concerned also about three passengers: Old Fire-Eyes Greco, the Great Doré, and the king.

Tuli had these biographies neatly arranged in alphabetical order. Having met with some mental difficulty in deciding where in alphabetical order to put the king, she had yielded to protocol and placed his biography on top. It was, in fact, no more than the formal entry in the *Galactic Who's Who;* and Claudine, skimming it swiftly and finding nothing more noteworthy than one would expect in the case of a ruler of a stable planet, passed on to the next ones.

Lieutenant Brh turned out to hail from the planet Galen, the only satellite of the little orange star Alshain. His cerise complexion and chunky stature were racial for Galen's dominant race. He was thirty-three years old. Having joined the Merchant Asterine at the age of eighteen, he had served competently on various starships and had joined the officer complement of the *Eiland* three years earlier, becoming third officer after a year. Nothing suspicious in his record. However, he had as police officer free access to the engine room; and he had been present at the death of Swainson, though not at the death of Schwarz.

Little was known about the Great Doré: no *Who's Who* entry, no police record, only a⋅brief biographical clip from the interplanetary theatrical paper *Drop Dead!* dated a year before when his act aboard the *Eiland* had been unveiled: evidently he had been too obscure for prior notices, and the tone of the article cocked an eyebrow at his abrupt rise to plush billing out of nowhere. (The short article was headlined: NIPPER FLIPPER CLIPPER SHIPPER.) His age would now be about thirty, he was unmarried, and except that he was a native of some undisclosed golden Ligerian continent, his origins were unknown. Claudine decided, with some regret, that the handsome, friendly, sharp-shooting, gunsight-transposing Doré must be kept under scrutiny, if only because he had been present at both deaths—concerning which, for purely intuitive reasons, she was growing increasingly suspicious. "Get more on him," Claudine commanded.

The notes about Old Fire-Eyes Greco she merely skimmed, knowing his lifetime of interplanetary apocalyptic activities fairly well; the police had kept good track of him, although his only offenses had been public-peace disturbances: a paranoid-at-large is always dangerous; it is only a question when the combination of grandeur delusions and persecution delusions, both born of deep-interred and redirected guilt, will convince him that he is pushed against a wall and must strike violently outward. Although he had not been present at the death of Schwarz, and apparently not at the death of Swainson, the captain's demise had occurred soon after the threatening appearance of Greco in the salon. Not only that, but Greco had predicted the space-death of the *Eiland of Ligeria*—at a time almost immediately following the discovery of the queer hue in the DM-component—and had actually called the ship a Sodom and Gomorrah! She could not imagine *how* Greco could have tampered with the mighty DM; but had he done so, or been involved in a leadership role, it would have been entirely within his personality structure to leave the cryptic sticker, *Sodim e Gomorrh,* as a dire clue to the agency of disaster. Of course, it was not yet known that there was anything wrong with the DM, no disaster might be impending; yet . . . Claudine was about to get out the sticker and discuss it with Tuli; then she looked at her wristwatch, shuddered, looked at her cutichron, and saw that there was not enough time before the captain's conference—she wanted first to go over all these biographies. Anyhow, keep Greco, too, up front for the time being.

Concerning Dr. Hastings there was a neat personnel abstract from Merchant Asterine files. From the time when he first earned his M.D., he had interned and residenced and served in the Merchant Asterine with moderate distinction and with no demerits or irregularities. He had published several medical papers and was not unknown among civilian doctors. Claudine quickly set that one aside.

Lieutenant-Commander Mashti, now acting captain, was characterized (this Claudine knew) as an indigo sapsucking Maruvian—Deneb Okab II. (Fascinating that among those of the crew who did not hail from Ligeria, a number had originated at other stars of the same constellation, Aquila!) Otherwise his biography was not dissimilar to that of Brh. Claudine, though, was definitely alert to Mashti, and she fruitlessly scrutinized the notes for some clue to suspicion. He had been present at both deaths; and, like Brh, he had access to the engine room. Furthermore, he struck her as an inadequate personality who had little chance at further promotion; and since there can be both paranoid and schizoid underlays to inadequate personalities, it was not inconceivable that Mashti might have imaged himself as profiting by the deaths of his two senior officers: should he bring in the *Eiland* with competency and even with distinction, it would certainly strengthen his career and might bring him immediate promotion. But how then he might see himself as profiting from disaster to the *Eiland,* involving his own death, was a bit inscrutable: inadequate personalities are not as a rule suicidal. Claudine muttered to Tuli: "I keep reminding myself that we may be merely borrowing trouble —*probably* both deaths were natural, and *probably* the DM-component is merely embarrassed because it is going to be reprocessed."

"Probably," Tuli responded, her lips tight: it was not clear agreement. In both their minds, Mashti joined Doré and Greco in top priority for close surveillance.

The last three in order were Schwarz, Suren, and

Swainson. Since two of these were dead, examination of their dossiers might seem unimportant—but not to Claudine and not to Tuli, because their files *might* provide possible *whys*. One glance at the multipage Schwarz dossier, however, told Claudine that it was for later when she had more time. Setting it aside, she held Suren in one hand and Swainson in the other. Ignoring Tuli's manifest disapproval, she went first to Swainson, wishing to spend more time on Suren.

As anticipated, Swainson's history was a variant of the Brh and Mashti histories: a good officer, indeed in his case an excellent officer—many years, many ships, everything regular, nothing to nudge a policeman's nose in the direction of a motive for killing him. And as for the DM-component—hadn't Swainson averred to Suren that Swainson, like Schwarz, knew a way to meet failure of the DM?

Possible motive for slaying Schwarz and Swainson both? *If* they had been slain?

Claudine spent five minutes incredulously reading and rereading the file on Commander Suren. His record was extremely unstable: how he had risen to the rank of engineering commander was only a little less understandable than how he had been chosen to fill the vacancy aboard the *Eiland* on her final voyage.

At length Claudine looked at Tuli. "What do you think?"

"He is a golden Ligerian," stated the chief glacially, "though that in itself means little; but he would have no reason to love the king. In terms of his job, he is the one who would be most competent to sabotage the DM, and the one who would have the best opportunity to do so. On the other hand, his general competency is open to question. But if in fact he were guilty, then he would have reason to kill Schwarz if he knew that the captain could overcome the malfunction, and later, reason to kill Swainson when Swainson said that *he* could. Besides, look at this item right here."

"Just a moment, I'm looking at *this* item right *here*." Claudine tore her eyes away from it: "What's yours?"

Tuli just pointed. Three years ago Commander Suren, on leave, had got himself arrested in the course of a golden Ligerian antiroyalty demonstration; and after being held for two days, he was released, no evidence having developed identifying him with the demonstration or its sponsoring organization. Suren had deposed that he was an innocent bystander caught in the police-mob action.

Claudine cleared her throat. "As you know, Tuli—no good in court."

"But good in police work."

"Maybe so—if it doesn't lead us off on a tangent."

"What were *you* looking at?"

"This one is just as esoteric as yours—maybe more so. Six years ago, Suren was transiently hospitalized and treated for nervous strain. The notation makes clear that he had been on prolonged rough duty."

"So?"

"Suren strikes me as a man who has depressive tendencies. This so-called nervous strain might have been mild reactive depression. I wish I knew."

"Why?"

"Any crew member or passenger who will sabotage his own ship in space has got to be willing to disintegrate with it. And a depressive can be suicidal. This you don't look for, by the way, in a man like Mashti, if I've sized him up right."

Silence.

Claudine stood, gathering up the papers. "That seems to do it for now, Tuli, except for the Schwarz dossier which I'll dream over tonight. Well done. Just now I have to go to a captain's call. You'll stay here and cover the king?"

"Of course. I—assume that door is locked from this side and unlocked from *his* side?"

"No, it is entirely unlocked."

Tuli's eyebrows hit ceiling.

"Keep it that way," added Claudine. "It's an honor thing."

Tuli's eyebrows departed randomly from each other as the phone chimed and Claudine went to answer it.

"Doré here," said the phone. Silence followed.

"Yes, Mr. Doré?"

Silence. Then, all in a rush: "Excuse me for disturbing you but you said I could call and so I'm taking the liberty of seeing if I can ask you. Asking if I can see you." Cough; then, very small: "O god."

Claudine rippled delighted laughter, pulled herself to a cheek-popping halt, and called out before he could get mad and disconnect: "The answer is yes—but I don't know when. This afternoon is took, and this evening looks grim, and in general I seem to be on active duty."

"I rehearsed that, you know."

"I know."

"Not well enough, though."

"Maybe you overtrained—some of your own flipping crept in. Listen, I'm on duty call right now. Where can I phone you?"

She heard breath sucked in. "You wouldn't!"

"Sure would."

"Before 1800 hours, right here, Room B-243, it's right off Frolic Street. After 2030, at the theater, backstage: I go on about 2130—two a day, you know. After 2230— well, B-243."

"If I don't call before 2230, I'll call tomorrow. Bye!" Disconnecting, she checked her watch, shuddered, checked her cutichron, and announced: "Taking off now, Tuli. I'm hard on the conference."

"Miss—"

"Yes, Chief?"

"I want to ask you something, but—just a moment—" Going to the phone, Tuli pushed the connect button, then pushed the disconnect, then turned to her officer. "I found out that the phones on this ship can be bugged by anybody who knows how. For instance, while you were talking to Mr. Doré, if he had held an electronic cigarette lighter against the transmitter while you disconnected, it would have disrupted the switch at this end so the line would have remained open."

71

"And he could then have been listening to our conversation?"

"Right."

"Oh, the depravity of it!"

"Right."

"But we don't know that he did this."

"Right. But anyhow, I killed the possibility by connecting and disconnecting again. That does it."

"So now you have a question to ask me."

Tuli wet her lips and blurted: "Do you want to tell me why you always shudder when you look at that wristwatch?"

"You won't tell anybody else? No, you won't. Here, look at it."

Tuli studied the Jaeger-LeCoultre. "It's pretty. What's wrong with it, except that it doesn't tell time right?"

"Tuli, Tuli!"

The chief looked at it again and frowned. "How do you tell seconds on this watch?"

"You can't, it has no second hand. It's a lady's watch, the theory is that we'd be late anyway. You have to watch the minute hand and estimate. Do that for about half a minute."

Tuli subsided into robotic study. At the end of the thirtieth second, she asserted: "The minute hand seems to be going backward."

"That's right."

"Did it always?"

"Not sure." Frowning, Claudine was scrutinizing the watch: it wasn't the first time she'd tried to remember. Up came her head: "Got to go, Tuli. Back-burner this one—it may mean something, though I'm blasted if I know what it would mean."

"Oh, Miss—"

"Tuli?"

"I meant to tell you. The assassin has escaped."

"Who?"

"The golden Ligerian we brigged for trying to knife the king. He's gone."

"When? How?"

72

"Disappeared early this morning. Nobody knows how. Cell door locked normally—but no prisoner."

Feet apart, hand on a hip, Claudine frowningly pulled at her lower lip. "Could be hazardous. What have you done?"

"With Lieutenant Brh, doubled the guard on this corridor—and one of ours is always present. Lieutenant Brh's people are on the lookout for the character."

Claudine spread hands. "Guess that's all we can do. Keep alert here, Tuli. See that system of three lights above the intercommunicating door? The first one is on: that means the king is in the salon. If the second one is on, he's in his bedroom. If the third one is on, he's somewhere else in the suite. It's automatic, he always wears the activator on his wrist. If all three are out, and you're still here, you've goofed: he's got clear away without you."

"How do I tell he's leaving?"

"Well, excuse me: if he gets away without you, *he's* goofed. He's supposed to open the door and let you or me know he's going."

Silence. Claudine started for the outside door. As she opened it, Tuli's response came, very faint: "He—opens the door?"

"That's right."

"Very well, miss."

Claudine left, grinning a little.

10

Acting Captain Mashti entered, and they arose. Mashti, who was perspiring, looked significantly at the first seat to the left of the captain's chair—the first officer's chair, occupied yesterday morning by Swainson and last night by himself; today it was going to sustain the solid beef of originally Third Officer Lieutenant Brh. Mashti then glanced at the chair beyond Brh, which yesterday morning had been his own: in front of this chair stood, a bit self-consciously, a slight young lieutenant just appointed acting third officer. Beyond *him* glowered little Commander Suren. All three men looked back at Mashti; then as one they swiveled their gaze to the empty captain's chair. Mashti sighed and took it. They all sat.

Mashti looked now to his right at Claudine and, beyond her, grave Dr. Hastings. He cleared his slender sapsucking throat lightly, almost subliminally; as the talk proceeded, the little infralaryngeal *hrmf* would keep softly and unevenly punctuating his contributions. We will ignore all his lisping and most of his *hrmf:* the reader may assume both, with regularity.

"We are all here," Commander Mashti began. "Good —I think. For the record, I now formally assume command: it will be entered in the log."

He looked around. They all stared at the table. Acting First Officer Brh raised his head to give his skipper a slight affirming nod, then looked down again.

"Well—" said Mashti, and *hrmfd,* and stopped.

Without looking up, Dr. Hastings inserted: "Captain, don't take our silence as rejection. We all respect your command, only—you know."

"Right," affirmed Suren. The others nodded.

Mashti's countenance blended relief and deepened concern. "The following," he said, "is not a joke. There's a classic murder story from twentieth-century Earth called *Ten Little Indians.* I feel like a character in it. Whoever is in command poles-over, aboard this ship."

Said Acting First Officer Brh, looking up with a hard frown: "Please break the circuit, Captain. If you don't, I'm next."

"Why?" Mashti demanded, leaning forward with both hands flat on the table.

Hoping that an officer would answer, Claudine looked around; but since they were all silent, she suggested softly: "Since I'm the professional cop here, I guess I should be the one to ask: what makes it seem to be murder, especially?"

Mashti said gloomily: "Dr. Hastings?"

Heads came slowly up, turned toward the doctor. His stayed down; but otherwise he sat erect, hands on the table like Mashti's. He began with a deep frown: "You aren't going to believe this."

"Say it!" commanded Mashti.

The doctor looked at the ceiling. "I purposely avoided slicing the hearts. I have been subjecting them to electromicroscopic structural analysis, analogous to the procedure that is used with stressed metals. Each heart shows the same kind of irregular stress lines."

Claudine said to him, just loudly enough for all to hear: "I am Dr. St. Cyr, a psychologist. You are sane. Say it."

All arms were on the table, all heads forward.

Hastings told the table drearily: "The structure of the stress lines can mean only one impossible thing. Both hearts appear to have turned inside-out—and then to have righted themselves again."

Out of the strangulated silence arose one clear dead voice. Commander Suren wanted to know: "How could a heart be turned inside-out without splitting it and snapping it off from its pipes?"

Dr. Hastings merely shook his head, stone-eyeing the table.

Mashti was beginning to quiver. Catching his eyes, Claudine frowned coldly and snapped: "You were about to say, Captain?"

The Maruvian caught hold of himself. "This," he temporized, making words, "is obviously beyond the immediate resources of any of us. I am consequently going to appoint a task force to investigate these murders. This force will consist of all officers present. Lieutenant Brh, you have been replaced as police officer by Lieutenant Redl there; but in view of your experience and your acting command seniority, you will command this task force. Commander Suren and Commander Hastings, both of you should be members ex officio: do you accept command by Lieutenant Brh?"

Hastings nodded. Suren bit: "No need to accept it—I've got it."

"Good," responded Mashti innocently. "Lieutenant Redl"—the young acting third officer met his eyes brightly—"as new police officer, you of course must be a member. Now, Lieutenant St. Cyr, you too should be a member, but I cannot properly command you except within the limitations that you understand. What do you think?"

Claudine said succinctly: "I suggest you attach me as a consultant."

"Mr. Brh?"

The lieutenant nodded.

"Good, that is it. Mr. Brh, add any member of the crew at your pleasure. Report as you see fit, but no later than 0900 tomorrow. Any contributions from anyone before dismissal?"

"Yes," replied Suren.

"Commander?"

"I have a report on the DM-component."

"Well?"

"It will blow."

Strained silence.

Brh broke tension by remarking: "If so, that obviates the need for this task force."

Claudine helped: "Say not so, Lieutenant. If only in the interests of science, should we not disintegrate *knowledgeably* into the—"

"Lieutenant!" shrilled Mashti, banging a fist on the table. Claudine went contrite. Brh favored her with a grim grin. Suren paid no attention.

"Now," said Mashti, voice under tenuous control, "please give us more details, Commander. I am fascinated by your new grasp of the situation, after your display of technical ignorance in front of Commander Swainson."

Suren shot: "Do *you* know what the trouble is, or how to fix it?"

76

Mashti's indigo darkened. "It is you who are the engineer. So talk."

Looking down, Suren mumbled: "So I've been doing my homework, Captain—it's a survival situation. Let me try to tell you—"

Suren picked words with care: as always, semi-popularized articulation was not easy for him. "The general purple hue has now resolved itself into a hard, bright violet core, only a few meters in diameter, at the heart of the red sphere. Radiological mass-tests show that the specific mass of this core is at least a thousand times greater than the specific mass of all the remaining DM-component. This fact, associated with other tests, establishes that the violet core is catabolium. Do you know what that is?"

All slowly shook their heads.

"Then do you know what elastium is?"

"Of course!" Mashti snarled while Brh nodded. "Elastium is the substance of the DM-sphere."

"But you still don't know catabolium?"

Comfortless silence.

"Oboy," Suren sighed. "What do you know about atoms?"

Silence thickened. Then: "I know some elementary stuff," Claudine ventured. "If atoms are pertinent, let's have it—but keep it for a layman."

"That isn't easy. Tell me your understanding of what an atom is."

"Atoms are the fundamental components of matter. There used to be only about a hundred kinds; but now, thanks to meddlesome humanity, there are nearly two hundred. Okay so far?"

"Go on."

"Every atom consists of a nucleus and anywhere from one to a large number of electrons whirling around the nucleus in orbits, like planets around a sun. The nucleus is tiny but massive—it has most of the mass of the atom. The electrons are bigger but practically weightless. The distance from the nucleus of each electronic orbit de-

77

pends partly on the repulsive energy of the electron and partly on the pulling power of the nucleus. Now I think you know all I know. Can you work with it?"

"Primitive theory," grumbled Suren, "but I can work with it. Did the rest of you understand it?"

"Of course," Mashti asserted. The others nodded.

"Then I'll start," declared Suren, "by telling you the atomic composition of the DM-component.

"The DM is a sphere of pure elastium, a synthetic element having an atomic weight of 547—double the weight of the heaviest natural atom known. This means it has an enormous cloud of electrons and is very large as atoms go. It is also very unstable, but the only thing that unsettles it is high velocity. At trans-light velocities, all but its innermost fourteen electrons are stripped away. This occurs in the atoms near the outer surface of the DM-sphere. The impoverished nuclei or ions that remain sink to the interior of the sphere, for elastium behaves rather like a fluid—heavy stuff sinks. Meanwhile, however, the whole sphere behaves somewhat like a self-feeding organism: new and complete elastium atoms are formed on the surface of the sphere from atmospheric nitrogen around it: thus the DM-sphere remains always the same size, but its mass increases with velocity. We keep replenishing the atmospheric nitrogen by synthesizing it from raw space. Follow me so far?"

Claudine nodded, but she added: "What happens when velocity decreases?"

"Process reversed. That's all you need to know."

"Sorry, Teach. Now what?"

"Besides whirling in orbits around the nucleus, electrons have spin, like a planet's day-and-night rotation. Did you know that?"

"No."

"They do. And in atoms of elastium, the fourteen innermost electrons must have a particular direction of spin. If they spin in another way, it changes the entire behavior of the atom. The wrong spin produces a different element called catabolium."

"That's what you said the violet core is."

78

Suren stared at her, gave her a curt nod, and proceeded. "During manufacture of an elastium DM-sphere, complex precautions are taken to assure that the spin on the fourteen electrons of the three inner shells is correct for elastium. If the wrong spin produces catabolium, the DM will go radiant."

Mashti shifted in his seat. Then the others did.

Claudine inquired: "How?"

"The direction of spin affects the dynamics between the thrust-energy of the electrons and the pull of the nucleus. In catabolium, instead of the remaining fourteen electrons holding orbit, they give up energy, releasing violet photon-glow, and fall into the nucleus. The result is an increasingly impacted nuclear core to the DM. When the mass goes critical, it goes radiant. And that's what we have aboard the *Eiland of Ligeria*."

Mashti demanded practically: "How will this affect the ship?"

Moodily Suren informed them: "When the DM goes radiant, the entire ship and all aboard her will together become—a star."

Muddled half-understanding blazed into hideous comprehension. A star is incandescent.

"I'm afraid," said Suren, talking with extreme difficulty, "that I have not been a very good engineer for a long time. I lost motive some years back. I have goofed through my biennial refresher courses. Therefore I have no business aboard the *Eiland*. Maybe it is a joint judgment on me and on the *Eiland* that I boarded her for a voyage involving a disaster which I of all the crew should be able to abort. However, that's done; and I was once a very good engineer indeed, particularly on theory; and the survival urge has got me digging pretty hard into old notes. So I can tell you just about exactly what is going to happen—but I still don't know any way to stop it.

"There is good literature on what happens when a DM goes catabolic. The theory is backed by laboratory work. By the grace of good factory inspection, it has never happened on a real ship—never before.

"When the DM goes radiant, the breeder capacity of the catabolium swiftly contaminates the entire ship and all aboard. Its effect is, that all atoms aboard—ship-structure and people-structure—recombine as catabolium atoms. The overall mass does not increase, because an early effect is to ruin the machines that generate nitrogen from raw space, so there is no new source of matter. Consequently the DM and the ship and all aboard begin to shrink in size, as the stripped catabolium ions move toward the center of each body. Meanwhile, the ship and all aboard emit a steady violet glow—the photons discharged as catabolium electrons fall back into nuclei.

"At this point, the ship is a low-grade violet star. But as the total mass grows more and more impacted, the glow increases to brighter levels of incandescence. When the whole ship becomes about the size of a football, it will shine a steady bright yellow-white. Because of the enormous mass of our DM-sphere, this shining may continue undiminished for ten, twenty, thirty years, while the starship continues in freefall through space—except in the unlikely event that it might collide with a star or planet: a star would consume it, but it would pass right through a planet and continue on its way, until it would ultimately go out like—"

Suren paused, looking for an adequate simile. Brh suggested low: "—like a fire-balloon at night?"

"Brh!" breathed Claudine, entranced.

He grinned sheepishly and tossed in a credit: "Your William James."

And then there was an electrified lull while realization seeped in.

Hastings broke it: obviously he was in profound disturbance. "Suren—you mean we are all going to *burn* to death?"

Suren was frowning. Unexpectedly he turned to Claudine, seeking help.

She squeezed out pertinent thoughts. "Eventually we'll burn, yes," she told Hastings, "but I don't think we'll know about it, from what Suren says. Offhand I would not think that we would feel pain while our atoms were

80

being changed to catabolium: our violet radiation would not involve heat, and the whole changing would be a generalized rather than a local or distinctive challenge to our pain endings and recognition centers. . . . What do you think, Suren?"

He nodded, his forehead deeply creased. "I don't know the psychology of it—but there was a human experiment."

"A—human experiment?"

His face was grotesquely bitter. "Too late I discover what a guy can know if he will only do his homework. Several years ago there was a worker in a DM factory who was dying of radiation sickness. He volunteered. So they put him in a room with a fabricated catabolium sphere, and they left him there until he started to glow violet, and then they took him out and got his report before he died. He reported euphoria."

"How's that?" asked Mashti.

Suren appealed to Claudine.

"Euphoria," she said quietly, "is a *good* feeling, an expansive feeling. Maybe he even felt a little bit like a god, Suren?"

The engineer was staring at her. Presently he nodded. "That's exactly what he said."

Claudine soberly folded hands on the table. "No pain, then," she judged. "Instead, exaltation. Then, as one's brain and other nerves rapidly mass themselves into impactedness—unconsciousness, suspension of animation, quiet death. And after death—when one has shrunk to the size of a grain of mustard seed—a kindling of oneself, along with the ship, to a decade of star-brilliance. And if one's soul has been released at death, one's soul may even be watching with aesthetic appreciation the radiance of its own abandoned body—"

"Miss St. Cyr!" raged Mashti. "Stop that nonsense!"

Hastings, who was perspiring heavily, quavered: "I want to hope that it is not nonsense."

Meeting Mashti's eyes implacably, Claudine asserted: "It does not sound to me like the murder of a ship. It sounds more like the apotheosis of a ship."

81

Brh whip-cut: "Do we therefore defend it?"

Claudine's head snapped around. "Of course not. If we all could choose it freely, then it would be defensible. But it is being imposed upon us."

"All right," said Brh.

Silence.

Brh turned to Suren. "How do you account for this perilous condition of our DM, Commander? Sloppy factory inspection?"

"I don't think so," the engineer responded. "It would be unbelievable. Manufacturing methods are keyed to produce the elastium spin and to prevent the catabolium spin. A few atoms are bound to happen-out catabolium —but a few aren't dangerous: it takes a critical cluster of at least a hundred thousand catabolium atoms to start breeding the reaction throughout the sphere. Automatic inspection instruments count catabolium development and halt production when a hundred such atoms have been detected; and this is supplemented by between twenty-seven and thirty-one human back-up inspection procedures. Not in the factory, Brh. Aboard ship."

"How?"

Suren swallowed and pressed forward. "This will sound wild, but it is the best I can offer. There are golden Ligerians who know how to move matter by force of mind. I have never run into one who could affect spin in atoms, mind you, but—" He stopped, his golden skin turning slightly greenish.

Hastings, lips tight, asserted: "Somebody inverted two hearts."

Silence.

Brh wondered in amazement: "You are suggesting that some mind aboard was powerful enough to convert that vast massive thing into—"

"Not quite," Claudine cut. "He said a hundred thousand contaminated atoms in one cluster would start a breeder reaction. So the mind would only have to convert one cluster of atoms. How big a cluster would that be, Commander Suren?"

The Ligerian thumb-forefingered small. "Less than a cubic centimeter."

Claudine and Brh looked at each other and nodded.

Brh demanded: "Commander, is it possible to reverse the reaction—to convert the catabolium back into elastium?"

"I don't see how. One would have to spring the electrons back out of an impacted mass of nuclei. In my opinion, Lieutenant—and Captain Mashti—this ship and all aboard have had it."

Mashti pounded on the table. "I won't accept this! You are all ordered to *think* of something!"

Brh tried. "Isn't it true that our increasing velocity is promoting the catabolium reaction?"

"Yes."

"What if we were to cut acceleration and go into free-fall?"

"Of course it would slow the reaction. But at our present velocity, continuing in freefall without change, it would take us a week to drift to Ligeria—and crush into the planet or bypass it forever. And even so, the catabolium will continue to breed faster and faster until it passes the point of no return."

"Then suppose we cut velocity and turn around right here and return to Earth. We could do this at a steadily diminishing velocity that would get us home in two days. Your opinion, Suren?"

He shook his head. "To do that, we would have to turn around and use the repulsors forward-on to brake ourselves. This would constitute braking acceleration—and the resulting shock to the unstable catabolium is unpredictable."

Mashti, partially recovered, broke in: "Suren, what is your judgment as to *when* the DM will go radiant, if we continue present acceleration?"

"Sir, no later than 1400 hours tomorrow, but probably no sooner than 1800 hours today—that is to say, in between three and twenty-three hours."

"No later than 1400 tomorrow. That is to say, about when we reach peak velocity."

"Right. As a coincidence."

"And if instead we cut acceleration and go into free-fall?"

Suren closed his eyes and calculated. Opening them, he stated: "Depending on whether the catabolium has passed the self-compression threshold, it may hold steady indefinitely. At least, its progress will be retarded. Taking the pessimistic view—we would have at least until 1200 hours tomorrow."

Claudine, eyes closed, murmured: "Twelve o'clock high. Man the lifeboats."

Appreciating her again, Brh murmured back: "At trans-light velocity, what would you use for lifeboats?"

Mashti angrily slapped the table. "Mr. Brh! Miss St. Cyr!" They hushed and turned his way. Mashti stood: "Then my decision is made. You will all keep these facts and this decision confidential. Mr. Suren, you will cut acceleration and go into freefall until further notice: the inertial shield will keep the passengers from noticing. Mr. Brh, your task force will include among its problems the problem of sabotage to the DM-component: you will look into everything that is the least bit amiss with this ship, ranging from the deaths to the malfunction of the DM, and including anything that may be discovered all the way down to rust on pipe joints. Meanwhile, Commander Suren, you will turn your primary attention to the problem of overcoming the malfunction in the DM. That is all. Formation—dismissed." He left the cabin.

Standing, they looked at each other. Then Brh said, firmly assuming command of the task force: "Skipper won't mind if we do our preliminary plotting here. Gentlemen, please be seated. Lieutenant St. Cyr, when I say gentlemen, I include you." He looked at her gravely: recognizing an experienced policeman, she nodded gravely, and sat with the others.

Except Suren, who stayed on his feet and snapped: "Excuse me, please."

Brh looked up at him—without hostility, but hard. "Why?"

"You heard what the captain told me to do."

Waiting just barely long enough to make it seem his own decision, Brh responded: "Excused. Come right back." He turned immediately to the others, ignoring the departing Suren, and stated: "This is investigation. The most experienced investigator present is Lieutenant St. Cyr. May we hear from you, miss?"

She said instantly: "You'll recognize, Mr. Brh, that the concerns of a crime investigator are the same as the concerns of a philosopher or a scientist or a newspaper reporter: the Five W's and How."

Brh looked quizzical. "Reporters, yes, but—scientists? philosophers?"

"Same concerns—all good inquiry. *Who. What. When. Where. Why.* And *How.*"

Suren, returning from the intercom, bit: "End of Lesson One."

Brh incised: "And I hope you learned it well, Commander. You're listening to a pro at her game—she'll listen to you at yours."

Shaking his head a little as he seated himself, Suren boredly swiveled it to Claudine.

She said mildly: "Don't let me create hostility here by sounding like a prof, Commander. You have your engineering systems, I have my investigating systems. Can we, you should excuse the reproductive reference, put them together for constructive issue?"

Suren's mouth went all twisty and broke into a grin which he instantly pulled in, going grim again. He nodded once.

Brh said: "Carry on, miss."

Claudine asserted: "The *who* and *why* are maybe the most important, but they aren't always the first facts to come out. So let's put them on the back burner and concentrate on the others. First: *what.*"

Brh summarized: "A lethal radiance buried in the DM-component, probably involving the whole ship long before this time tomorrow, no known way to stop it. Two successive captains successively and suddenly dead of mysteriously inverted hearts—without snapping off the

85

pipes. By the way, gentlemen—in case any of you wonders whether I am pursuing this matter with a whole heart —if Mashti gets it too, I replace him in the death seat. Did I mention a whole heart?" Pause for effect: no sound. "Go on, miss."

Claudine doggedly pursued it, but without revealing more of her own thinking than she had to. "Eventually we start hunting around for connections between the deaths and the DM, but of course they may not be connected. And then again, they may be. But I think next we ought to consider the *how*." She looked at Suren: "Commander, you said the sphere was converted psychokinetically from elastium to catabolium. Is that right?"

Again he was surly. "It *was* elastium. It *is* catabolium. How, I don't know. Not factory. So maybe PK."

Claudine let her eyes pensively dwell upon him. Then she shook her head as though to shake off her concern with him; and she turned to Commander Hastings and demanded: "Doctor—*how* could a heart get inverted— and then reinverted to normal form? Especially, how without—what did you say, Commander Suren?"

"Mmf?"

"A little while ago—you expressed it so well!"

"Expressed what?"

"Wait . . . eh, *yes,* Commander! You asked: 'How could a heart be turned inside-out without splitting it and snapping it off from its pipes?' Doctor?"

Hastings ran a hand through his graying hair. He responded: *"Or* would be better than *and."*

"Pardon?"

"I could maybe somehow invert a heart without snapping its pipes if I split it—or without splitting it, although God knows how, if I could snap its pipes. But these hearts were not split—and they did not snap their pipes. And I don't know how they inverted without either splitting or disconnecting; but for that matter, I don't know how they inverted at all. I only know that they *have* to have been inverted—it's the only explanation of the stress-lines."

Claudine brooded. Then she looked at Brh.

Again he summarized: "So we know the *what,* and we all will investigate the *how,* and we have back-burnered the *who* and *why.* Well, miss?"

"It's well worth while," she observed, "to pay attention to the *when.* The *wheres* we know exactly, and some of the *whens;* but let's try to nail down the exact timetable.

"We were airborne before 1000 hours yesterday morning. About 1300 hours, Commander Suren noticed the peculiar hue of the DM-component. Shortly after 1400 hours, a golden Ligerian mountebank tried to knife the king—"

"You know he's at large?" interrupted Brh.

"I know."

"Go on."

"During dinner, along about 1930 hours, a disturbance was created by that wild paranoid Fire-Eyes—"

"Eh?" Hastings interjected.

"Fire-Eyes. Greco."

"You said paranoid."

"Well, I suppose I did. It's pretty obvious, isn't it?"

"Well, yes." Hastings looked about. "She's *Doctor* St. Cyr, a psychologist."

Brh commented. "Good—that should help with the *why.*"

When they were quiet, watching her, Claudine glided on. "Old Fire-Eyes threatened doom, and was dragged out." (She made a quick decision to avoid mentioning, quite yet, either *Sodom and Gomorrah* or *Sodim e Gomorrh.*) "A few minutes later, Captain Schwarz dropped dead—from an inverted heart. After that, nothing happened until about 1000 hours this morning, when Captain Swainson dropped dead—from an inverted heart. And there has been nothing since—has there?"

They brooded.

Claudine, exasperated, demanded: "Is Old Fire-Eyes the *only* one on this ship who can qualify as a goofy suspect? Does it *always* unimaginatively have to be a paranoid?"

They brooded.

Brh cleared his throat and suggested: "If nobody has

anything constructive to add at this time, I suggest we move out on our several natural task-force roles. Dr. Hastings, please consider the medical implications and anything else that may occur to you. Commander Suren, kindly proceed with investigations in your own department, and also conduct a complete mechanical inspection of the ship—to the last detail. Miss St. Cyr, you are on your own. Lieutenant Redl, you will work with me on the police details of the problem. Are we ready to break up?"

Redl wet lips and said: "I have something—"

"Yes, Mr. Redl?"

He was a dark young Bavarian, and there was the very slightest thickening of his English. "You know," he began diffidently, "I am also communications officer."

"My sympathies, Mr. Redl—we are all doubling up. And?"

"Just prior to the captain's call, we had a top-secret idaradiogram from Galactic Headquarters—"

He shriveled as all heads slowly swiveled his way. Brh said incisively: *"Yess,* Mr. Redl?"

The Bavarian cleared his throat and blurted: "A coalition of white and golden Ligerians have overthrown the planetary government and installed a junta which claims to speak for the planet."

The silence was turgid.

Brh said softly: "It would have been dandy of you to mention this with the captain present—an hour ago, Mr. Redl."

The third officer's jaw stiffened. He shot: *"When,* Mr. Brh?"

Brh looked at Claudine for help. She spread hands and fingers. The Brh mouth spread a little in a fate-mocking grin. "All right, Lieutenant Redl—I don't suppose either Mashti or I gave you much chance to talk. But, man, you're an officer—next time it's hot, *barge* in!" He turned again to Claudine, grin spreading: *"Next* time, I said— you heard that, didn't you? All right, Claudine—what do we do now?"

She appreciated his "Claudine" in the thickening gloom of the news. She asserted: "It means we can't land on

88

Ligeria—even if we had a chance of getting there. It means the king is no longer king—even if he lives. It means a change in flight plan—if there is any point in flight plans. I can tell you two things, Brh—the captain and the king must be told immediately—and nobody else must be told."

Silence.

Redl cleared his throat and added: "There was also something about assassins everywhere, waiting for the king."

"That," said Brh, "could be our *why*."

II

After the conference broke, Claudine avoided her stateroom: too close to the king—especially while he was being surprised by Mashti with distressing information. Instead, she went to a place where she could maybe think: the observation point where she and the king and Captain Schwarz had watched the submarine take off. There were a few people in the large salon, but not many, and none whom she knew. Alone at a table somewhat back from the star-filled picture window in the hull bow, she ordered small beer and meditated.

For a little while she studied the stars ahead: it was good for composure. A very large segment of the sky— much more than from Earth—was filled by the wing-spread constellation Aquila the Eagle—his beak orange with the star Tarazed, with blinding white Altair (their prime target) marking his left shoulder and little orange Alshain halfway down the leading edge of the same wing; all the way across the eagle's body, yellow-white Deneb Okab nestled in the armpit of his right pinion; and dozens of apparently smaller stars—some named, some merely numbered—some really smaller, others only seeming smaller because they were hundreds of parsecs more distant, framed by the eagle in this perspective but not possessed by him. Droll that once she would attain to that constellation, it would cease to be a constellation! When, once in that constellation. she would be scanning the Ligerian night sky in search of Old Yellow Sol—in what sort of constellation would she be finding *him?*

Only she wouldn't be going to Altair now, would she? Even if the king should elect to enter the den of his enemies, the starship *Eiland* would forestall him by turning into a new little star.

Grim whimsy: in what constellation?

Answer: in one constellation after another.

It was her business, of course, to do what she could to prevent that same stardom—mainly for two thousand passengers and crew, partly to give the king an option. Well, of course, also to give *herself* a few options. Just how she was going to go about saving the ship with skull-work was another thing. Matters were just a bit more concrete than they had been before the conference: the infernal agency was now known to be catabolium, and the speculation was that the DM-sphere had been converted into a star-core by psychokinetic means. The catabolium at first had been only diffusely centered, not visible as such; but as the mass of the sphere had increased, the growing concentration of catabolium at the center had first produced the generalized purple hue and then at climax would glow incandescent-angry. Well, so much for a possible MO: finding somebody who *could* do it, and somebody who could do who *would* do, was the first impossible problem—and the next one, given that he might be found, would be to persuade him to undo what he had done. She shivered: it was probably too late even for the arch-criminal to unscramble this egg of cataclysm.

Theoretically the list of suspects could be narrowed to just those people who were able to flip matter; for even though someone else might have the motive and the master mind, he would require a master flipper for his agent.

90

Only, how could you tell who was a flipper, for precisely the guilty person would be the one most unlikely to flaunt his ability. She recognized that she was confronted by an unlikely series of three perfect crimes—two murders and ship sabotage, all utilizing in principle the same MO, none provable on circumstantial evidence.

During her conference with Tuli, four persons had emerged vaguely as semi-prime suspects for various vague reasons. Old Fire-Eyes Greco had a warped motivational pattern that would fit, but no access and no known flippability. (He was, however, known to be a master hypnotist, although that ability wasn't psychokinetic.) Mashti could have a motive and did have access, but he probably couldn't flip. Suren could have a motive and did have the best access of all; besides, as a golden Ligerian he might hate the king and maybe could flip. As for the Great Doré—she chuckled; for although he was the only one *known* to be a flipper, he had no access and no evident emotional pattern that would provide motivation; not only that, but of all possible suspects he would be the least suspect, since *he did* flaunt his ability—on stage!

. . . unless, of course, he should turn out to be an egomaniac who would actually enjoy being exposed, would bask in the theatrical notoriety of his own *Götterdämmerung*. . . .

. . . or turn out to be the naive tool of somebody with motive, such as Mashti or Suren or Greco. . . .

Patiently she checked it. All had to be filtered before names could be allowed to stick out like sore thumbs, distracting attention from the seat of disease. It was time to consider the possible *whys*—the range of pertinent motivation—the kind and condition of *mind* that would choose to commit these three entirely deliberate crimes. Not rational motives only: personality structure entered in. Intuitively now she was sure that the same person or the same team *had* committed all three—that all three were intrinsic to the same controlling motive—that, finally, the murders of the captains were subordinate to the murder of the ship. (Incidentally, Mashti could feel safe—one way or another, he would survive to die with

91

his ship: either he was the criminal, or there was no evident reason to kill him.)

The *crime passionel* possibility could be ignored unless something turned up. Unlikely that all three—Schwarz, Swainson, and the *Eiland*—had been targets of the same lover's jealousy!

She raised a finger, and more beer came automatically: it was two percent stuff, provoking only thought. The *ambition* motive made some sense, if you overlooked the DM. Somebody, poling-over captain after captain, might be grotesquely hoping to come into his ship kingdom. That, of course, practically eliminated all but the top officers. Mashti? even Suren? she'd been over this ground with Tuli. On this showing, she mirthlessly reflected, Mashti if guilty was on a spot: he could evade suspicion only by dying.

Ambition, though, hardly encompassed the violet DM-core and the death of a ship with all passengers and crew. If you posited that Mashti wished to die spectacularly in command, you had to show that Mashti was this kind of guy—and he didn't seem to be, although who could tell about an indigo sapsucker?

No: rather the concept of star-murdering a spaceliner looked more like the apocalyptics of Fire-Eyes Greco. *Sodim e Gomorrh!* Just as soon as she broke this brood —at the end of this beer—she *must* get the facts about *that* detail! The little slender paper label had not been hand-fabricated, but rather, elaborately printed with enamel inks—costly, implying quantity production. Conceivably Greco had spent time in some nation of some planet—Ligeria?—where Sodom and Gomorrah translated into this: with financial backing, he had got perhaps tens of thousands of these printed and went sticking them everywhere. . . . Only, while he was at it, why hadn't he used presensitized adhesive? This label had been hand-glued to the lattice under the DM, apparently it hadn't even been primitively pre-gummed. Now whom could she ask about *Sodim e Gomorrh,* to be sure that it wasn't just one of those translingual coincidences having totally different meaning? The king? Maybe, if nothing else turned up by tomorrow; but somehow intuition told her that she shouldn't, just yet. And certainly not any of the top officers, all of them being under one or another degree of suspicion. Solution: put Tuli on it. . . .

However, the thought that it might indeed be Greco was attractive if trite. Psychologically, Greco fitted: he would deliberately leave the paper as a warning—even as an advertising signature, for one who could interpret it; but his paranoid cunning would cause him to hide it far down under the DM where it might not be discovered—except, of course, by a soul like her own, ripe for destruction, so twisted that she would be looking down there. How Greco could have arrived at getting loner-time in the engine room with the DM-component was a bit of a puzzler, but no reason to eliminate him yet. And one could tie in the command murders with the apocalyptic motive, making it all one pattern of Supernal Judgment on the frivolous *Eiland*. Yes, motives fitted Fire-Eyes fine; only—could he flip?

Whoever it might be had a fine sense of suspense. Who knew whether Mashti would drop dead, or when? and now, with acceleration cut and the ship in freefall, who knew when or if the DM and the ship would go radiant?

Radiant . . .

She was gazing at the TV screen above the picture window: the screen that revealed to her, externally, all of the *Eiland of Ligeria* as though the ship were distant from her, and she floating in space. With apprehension she surveyed the beautiful *Eiland* whose white twin hulls and superstructure filled more than half the screen, shining as though some star were nearby though none was near, while all around and behind her was star-punctuated blackness. . . . Then, in her imagination, the ship's color suddenly changed, going from normal white to ghastly violet, while the light that illuminated her seemed now to come from within. And then it seemed that the ship was receding from her, or she from it, going away into distance; but her brain knew that what her imagination was watching was the minimization of the ship as it catabolically shrank and all its people shrank and grew massive.

And when the ship seemed no larger than a remote football in space, it flared a blinding yellow-white. . . .

She tossed off the beer and stood. It fitted the mind who had sabotaged the *Eiland*—Greco or another—first, that he would make the suspense real by letting it be known all over the ship; and second, that he would make *himself* known. And he had not done either. . . .

"NOW HEAR THIS!" She froze: a high baritone was horning out of the squawk-box, filling the salon. "This is NOT the captain! Hearken again to me, ye befouled swine of Sodom and Gomorrah! Ye shall die in the Holy Fire!"

Claudine and the few other people in the salon swung round to the squawk-box as though it had activated all of them in a mechanical drill routine. Claudine, trained for voice-recognition, knew it instantly: Old Fire-Eyes; his enormously tall, stringy, ragged, bearded figure rose up in her hintermind. Now *how* in the *hell* had he . . .

"Listen ye!" Greco bawled. "Every man and woman on this ship hears my voice, except only the many who are drunk and the two who are slain. As for the drunken, tell them, tell them, ye who are sober at the moment! As for the slain, remember them! Your captain is dead: you know that, but do you know *how?* GAWT struck him dead! Your first acting captain is dead, too: GAWT struck him dead! They were signs, *signs:* not terminations, not ends in themselves, but the *finger writing on the wall!* And what the finger hath writ is this: SODOM AND GOMORRAH—ALL ON THE SHIP SHALL DIE—AND THE SHIP HERSELF IS A HARLOT WHO SHALL DIE IN SPACE FOR HER SINS!"

They were all on their feet: you couldn't sit. Claudine wanted to run for the Command Area to case the situation—but she had to hear the end of this clearly.

"Listen ye! *I* am your captain now! I am Greco—an instrument of Gawt, a voice and hands for Gawt! *I* command this ship! And I command each and every one of you to go to your cabins and pray! *pray!* PRAY! But pray not for bodily salvation, for nothing shall save this ship, Gawt hath doomed this ship and every soul aboard!

94

I shall not tell you the hour of her doom: I know what it is, but Gawt hath commanded me not to tell: doom shall strike when it striketh, and each of ye shall die! So pray not for the salvation of your bodies; but pray, pray desperately, with deep intercessive prayer, for the salvation of your slimy souls! Go to your cabins and pray! *Go!* GO—"

There was a background crash, and incongruously the Voice of Doom blurted "Oh, damn!" and went strangulated. A moment later somebody killed the intercom.

Claudine, batting aside two other women who were fleeing the salon in panic, started on an indecorous run for the Command Area. Then it *was* Old Fire-Eyes: he *knew* about the murders, he *knew* about the DM-component, he *had* alerted the whole ship, he *had revealed himself:* his motives were perfectly clear—violent guilt-projective paranoid psychosis! All that really remained to be demonstrated was the *how* involving the *when;* and that would all come out under her questioning, she knew how to handle these lonely-unhappy guys. . . .

But could she handle him well enough to get him to *save* the ship?

Could he still save her. . . .

12

Swinging around an intersective corner, she ran hard into a big male back. Nobody fell, but he swung and caught her around the waist as she grabbed his shoulders. "Well!" gasped the king, his eye-corners crinkling with pleasure.

She gasp-grinned back, then clung to him, face against his chest, while she recovered. A moment later she moved away and looked up at him, deadly serious. "Let's go!" she commanded, and hooked his arm and spun him around to move him on. . . .

The squawk-box clicked on, and Mashti's lisping voice asserted: "Now hear this." She stopped the king to listen. With a self-controlled calmness that overjoyed her, Mashti said: "This *is* the captain. I am Acting Captain Mashti, Lieutenant-Commander Mashti, now correctly addressed as *Captain* Mashti. I was second officer until the unhappy deaths by heart attack—*by heart attack*—of Captain Schwarz and First Officer Swainson. We have an overexcited passenger in custody here, unfortunately he is very ill, you have heard him raving, we will see to his treatment. You can disregard everything he said, except that of course prayer never does anybody any harm."

The little *hrmfs* were in the background; now Mashti paused, indulged in a big *hrmf,* and launched into a speech. "I hope now that all of you are seated, unless you prefer to stand. Our prisoner here is Mr. Greco; some of you know him as Fire-Eyes. Mr. Greco is well known on several planets for extreme incitive behavior. I—ah— well, your acting captain has to confess that he is a bit embarrassed and at a loss as to how Mr. Greco passed our normal guards, gained access to the master intercom, and drew off the crewman who was on duty; at any rate, Mr. Greco locked himself in here, and you heard what he had to say.

"I want to reassure you categorically on all counts. First, both Captain Schwarz and First Officer Swainson had been under extreme stress for prolonged duty-periods, and the doctor has given me no *hrmf* evidence to show that their heart attacks were in any way *hrmf* unnatural. Second, at the risk of some immodesty, I should point out that I have commanded a number of smaller ships, and have my master's papers, and have served as second officer aboard this ship for three years in the full confidence of Captain Schwarz; my regular and frequent duties have entailed active and full operative command of this ship for periods of many hours; and there is absolutely no reason for anyone to have the slightest lack of confidence in my competency to command her for the duration of the voyage and to bring her in with luxurious *expertise;* for that matter, the former third officer who is now my first officer, Senior Lieutenant Brh, can do the same if necessary. So as far as the crew of this ship is concerned, the voyage is just as it was before the first incident, other than our natural mourning of the untimely passings of Captain Schwarz and Commander Swainson.

"Finally, this business about a doomed ship is the imagining of a mentally ill man. I can say this with full confidence, because since the death of Captain Schwarz, Commander Swainson and then myself have required and conducted the fullest inspection of this ship in its minutest details, a thing you'd expect us to do as captains assuming command.

"My recommendation to all of you is: make this a *memorable* voyage, a *pleasure* voyage! We regret and mourn the deaths of our masters—but there is an appointed time for each of us to die, and the world goes on, and so they would want it. Especially Captain Schwarz, who loved the *Eiland of Ligeria* with all his heart, wished with all his heart that her final voyage to her name-planet would be an occasion of unparalleled jollity and merriment. I commend to all of you that you will remember him best with joy.

"This—is *the captain.* Out."

It clicked off. The king and Claudine were profoundly moved, they were clasping four hands tightly. After a moment, they recovered.

"That should do it," the king commented.

Claudine nodded tightly and pulled him forward.

All along, she had been conscious or semiconscious that Chief Tuli had been shadowing the king. It transiently reassured her, although she really didn't need the reassurance, having total confidence in Tuli; nevertheless she always felt faintly guilty when she was not herself physically guarding the king.

The scene in the Communications Cabin was classic. Fire-Eyes was trussed in a chair, glaring through a blindfold. Flanking him were two bored, armed crewmen. A little distant, a clutch of officers argued, with Lieutenant Redl centrally and maximally excited. (It was his cabin.)

Claudine suggested to the king and the chief: "You guys drift in behind the officers. I want to work on the beast."

She went over to Fire-Eyes and stood directly in front of him. Through his blindfold she felt the muffled force of his eyes. She put arms akimbo and glared back. His blindfold wavered away. She relaxed, clasping a wrist with a hand in front of her, feet apart a little. Greco looked up at her again—still glaring, but staying with her.

"Want to talk?" she demanded.

He turned his head away as though bored.

Behind her, Redl babbled: "As nearly as I can figure out, he hypnotized the guard and got into this intercom control room and hypnotized the duty-man and locked the door. Suren here stumbled on the situation by the purest accident—the guard was a zombie—so Suren kicked in the door and got Greco before Greco could get him."

Claudine glanced at Suren. He was glowering by a wall.

Brh bit: "Some sick man. He damn near took over the ship—or threw it into a convulsion, anyway. Skipper, you did a good job on that recovery."

Mashti, behind her with Redl, toothlessly snapped: "He's obviously guilty as hell—the whole complex. Question him, miss!"

Claudine objected: "I can't question a blindfolded man. It is contrary to police ethics."

"Unblindfold him, then!"

Brh interjected: "Wait! If you do that, he'll hypnotize all of us and get away!"

"Hear that?" demanded Mashti. "If we unblindfold him, you can't question him for sure. So question him blindfolded!"

"Sorry," said Claudine, reaching out to fool with the knot on the eye bandage, behind Greco's head.

Behind her she sensed a multiple backward cowering,

and she correctly guessed that the cowerers were Mashti, Redl, and Suren. Nevertheless she removed the blindfold and confronted the naked fire-eyes of Greco.

After a moment of silence, Redl muttered: *"Höllenfeuer!"*

Claudine raised her voice a little. "No sweat, gentlemen: I gave him a fix with a neck nerve back here, and now *he* is hypnotized—within limits. I'm a pro, he's an amateur: he'll do anything with hypnotism, I won't. Mr. Brh, are you familiar with the legal limits?"

"I am," said Brh, who was now the only one right behind her.

"Did all the rest of you hear that question and answer?"

They affirmed, diversely.

"Now therefore all of you are witnesses to what is done here, and Mr. Brh will be witness to its legality. Mr. Greco, can you hear me?"

"I can." Greco's voice sounded normal for a human, although subdued for Greco.

"I am a police officer, and I am about to question you. Do you understand this?"

"I do."

"Tell me what your rights are."

"I—I do not know them, for sure."

"That is a lie, you've been challenged by more policemen than I have. What are your rights, Mr. Greco?"

He wet lips and responded: "I do not have to answer without benefit of counsel."

"That is right, Mr. Greco. And you do not now have benefit of counsel—so you do not have to answer. But I have hypnotized you, a little. Tell me—are you able to inhibit answering?"

"Yes."

"Do you have to tell the truth if you do answer?"

"No."

"Are you able to positively lie?"

"Yes."

She turned to Brh. "Lieutenant, in your opinion, are we within the legal limits?"

99

"In my opinion, yes." Brh was fascinated.

"Gentlemen, you are all witnesses to my question and Mr. Brh's answering opinion. I will now proceed with questioning—"

Mashti burst out: "This is nonsense! If your hypnosis is no good, what good is your hypnosis?"

"It is quieting." She found a little chair, pulled it up, and sat on it, knees apart and folded hands between them, leaning forward toward him. "I heard you on the intercom. What a marvelous voice!"

He squeezed his eyes shut.

"I won't ask you if you meant all you said—I know you were being totally honest. But I do wish I knew what you meant."

His eyes reopened, he stared at her insolently. "It is for each of you to judge. If Gawt is with you, the truth will come into you."

She bowed her head. "I know. But some of us are too sinful for God to enter us. And yet we know we are sinners, and we wish that we could find our way to God. Can you help me?"

His gaze triflingly softened. "Woman, do you confess that you are a sinner?"

"I do."

"And you realize that you can never find grace, because Gawt has predestined you to Hell?"

"This too I realize. And yet—I should like maybe to stop short at Purgatory. Can you help me?"

"You really *want* help?"

She met his eyes soberly. "I really want help."

His eyes went crafty. "As a woman—or as a police officer?"

She replied candidly: "I am questioning you as a police officer—but as a woman, if you have any help to offer, I shall be glad of it."

Suren muttered: "Damn!"

Reaching out with a long arm, Greco placed a hand on her head. "Will you confess your sins to me?"

Making her mouth very small, she demurred; "Do not

100

tempt me, sir. We Protestants should confess our sins only to God."

His hand wavered away, he folded it on the other hand, but he was definitely interested. He said quietly: "And you *are* confessing them to Gawt?"

"I am," said Claudine. And she was. Inwardly she was saying: "Dear God, I know five sins, and for these I am sorry, and for the others that I did not recognize I am sorry too, whatever they were."

Fire-Eyes leaned soft-eyed forward and took both her little hands in his big hands. "Then," he asserted, "I can help you, my daughter. What guidance do you want?"

Her eyes on his eyes were very large. "I have to know, sir. Exactly how did God punish the captain and the first officer?"

"By striking them dead, Daughter."

"But *how* did He strike them dead? Did He strike them in the head with His lightning?" Somehow she got the pronouns orally capitalized.

"It is not for us to know. I do not know myself. He struck them—that is enough for us to know."

Inhibiting herself from glancing back at Brh, she pressed: "Do you *know*—or is this a guess?"

He stared at her. "It was revealed to me."

Her head dropped. "All right, Father—this I accept." Up came her eyes again: "But, Father—you said that the ship was doomed. *How* is it doomed, dear Father?"

"I do not know, my daughter." His voice had gone ineffably kindly. "I only know that this ship *is* doomed. Gawt does not tell me all that he knows, but this much he has told me."

Oh, damn! But she tried one more gambit: "Do you know *when,* my father?"

He patted her hand slowly, nodding his head slowly, holding his eyes on her eyes. "It will be before this ship reaches Ligeria. That is all I know, Daughter. Tell it to the others. Your sins are forgiven."

"Can you think of any reason, Father, why this ship should change course and steer for some port other than

101

Ligeria?" Did he somehow know about the revolution? How much did his Gawt let out?

He replied soberly: "Gawt has said nothing to me about that. And since the ship will die in space anyway, I do not suppose that it matters."

"Once more—you realize that I am a police officer questioning you?"

"Yes, my daughter. And I see you also as a troubled woman."

"Thank you. But since I am a police officer—do you wish to change anything you have said?"

"Why should I, my daughter? I have never lied."

"But you *can* lie if you choose—even though I have hypnotized you?"

"Certainly."

"Prove it by lying now. What is your name?"

"Rumpelstiltzkin."

Nobody laughed. Pressing his hands with a feeling not far from affection, Claudine sincerely demanded: "May I talk to you again?"

"Of course, dear."

Freeing her hands, Claudine smiled warmly. And then she got up and faced the officers. "I am amazed," she cried indignantly, "that you would harry this holy soul! What are your plans for him *now,* pray tell me?"

There was a shuffling silence. Then Suren truculently blurted: "The brig, until we find out what he's up to."

Claudine bristled: "I resist this! Do not confine this saintly man to the brig! Place him in quarters that he deserves!"

Mashti inserted: "Name other quarters that he deserves."

Turning, Claudine again seized the prisoner's hands, and flashed him a smile, and swiveled her head around to the captain. "Dr. Hastings has a private room off the sick bay. How about that?"

Within her hands, the prisoner's hands fluttered a moment, then stilled.

Mashti turned to Brh. "Okay?"

"Affirmative."

"Blindfold him first," Mashti ordered. "The Curse of St. Cyr could wear off." He signed to the crewmen, who blindfolded the prisoner and engaged his arms. Fire-Eyes left without protest.

Silence.

Mashti said: "It's a small table you have here, Mr. Redl—but let's sit around it."

They took chairs and scrounged up to it.

Mashti demanded: "Miss St. Cyr—what conclusions did you draw from the questioning?"

She frowned down. "There were none that I could draw. If we believe that he was telling the truth, then his guess that the murders were murders was a guess, and his guess that the ship is doomed was a guess, and he is projecting these guesses as divine revelation, and he believes all this. And he professed ignorance of the Ligerian revolution—which we have kept secret. If he is telling the truth, he is innocent. If he is lying, still he may be guilty. My procedure allowed him to lie. His personality structure makes him a motivational natural for this criminal series—but I do not see any way that he could have accomplished any of it."

"In short," snarled Mashti, "you defend him."

"In short," retorted Claudine, "my mind stays open, and he remains a prime suspect."

The king interjected: "I should like for *Doctor* St. Cyr to explain *why* he remains a prime suspect."

Mashti nodded.

"On the count of motive," she explained, "psychologically there is plenty of *why* for the hypothesis that either he did it or he masterminded it. He is paranoid, and the structure of his paranoia is apocalyptic: he is Gawt's instrument for vengeance, and he has labeled this pleasure-ship 'Sodom and Gomorrah'—"

"Pardon?" Suren interjected.

"Sodom and Gomorrah. In Earth's Judaic-Christian Bible, they were twin pleasure-cities which God destroyed by fire because of their sinfulness. The *Eiland,* by the bye, has twin hulls."

Suren stared. Then he said merely: "Okay. Go on."

Later, Claudine would remember that. Just now, filled with her theme, she pressed: "Greco's complicated symbolic mind would be capable of successively destroying Schwarz and Swainson—the captains, one by one—as divine signs: if you've read your Holy Scripture from any planet, gentlemen, divine pre-signs are usually inscrutable, their reasons hard to fathom because they are too esoteric to constitute effective specific warnings. Meanwhile he goes about his prime task: the destruction, or apotheosis, of the ship and all aboard, including himself as a sacrificial martyr—*that* prospect would lend his project *extra* energy! And it is psychologically consistent that he chose the method of the self-adjusting catabolium: the logic of the paranoid is intricate and compulsive—it would make divine sense to Greco that precisely by increasing her own velocity the *Eiland* would destroy herself, that her fiery self-destruction would occur precisely at the instant when she reached her maximum velocity, symbolizing the apex of her sinful arrogance.

"Partially validating this, I had predicted that the criminal would announce the crime to the whole ship, which Greco did; and that he would reveal himself to the whole ship, which Greco did. And the key point—the one that turned my thoughts definitely his way—is the fact that he *labeled* the two deaths as murders, Gawt's judgments, coupled with the fact that he *knew the ship was doomed.*"

She paused, spreading hands. "But under questioning, he evaded all pertinent issues. And in the spirit of honest inquiry, I have to admit that this same personality structure would allow him, quite coincidentally, to *conclude* that the deaths were God-strikings, and to *wishfully predict* that the ship would die. So where are we?"

She waited.

Mashti pressed: "Are you ready to accuse him?"

"No."

"Why not?"

"First, because we are still vague on the *where* and *when:* if we put it that Greco is guilty, still we don't know when he got into the engine room, and we have to admit that he had been removed from the dining salon when Schwarz died, and we don't know that he was present when Swainson died. Second, because of the *how*— the MO: we have no knowledge that he is capable of inverting hearts or changing electronic spin."

Mashti thundered: "He can hypnotize!"

"So can I—but I can't flip. They aren't the same. I was going to go on and mention the third difficulty. In the midst of our anxious concerns, let's pause to appreciate the following fact aesthetically: here we have what amounts, not merely to a perfect crime, but to a perfect crime *series*. We have no physical clues, other than knowledge that flipping was involved—and how do you learn whether a suspect can flip? And if he can, can he flip that well?" *She* had maybe a physical clue—*Sodim e Gomorrh*—but she wasn't ready to unveil it. "These crimes," she concluded, "cannot, in any way that I can see, be proved without a confession *plus* our very indirect collateral evidence."

Brh leaned forward. "But if you could prove all these other matters, the circumstantial evidence would by its own weight lead a military court to convict him without a confession "

"Granted. But the court would be wrong. He could die protesting innocence, and doubt would remain. And this, gentlemen, is about as perfect as a crime can get to be. Aesthetically, I mean."

"Well," asserted Mashti sensibly, "now that we art-lovers have appreciated beauty, I suggest a concern more immediate than court conviction. We want to avoid being extinguished. So we need to find the criminal, so we can try to make him neutralize his own bomb. Lieutenant St. Cyr, what primarily do you need in order to force Greco to spill the beans?"

"Knowledge that he can invert—or owns an inverter."

"And your plans?"

"If I may be excused, Captain, I am going to make a date with the Great Doré."

"Who's he?"

"The professional flipper at the Frolic Street theater."

"Why?"

"Some of my reasons could be inferred from my recent remarks. For present purposes, let's merely say that I need to know more about flipping, and he is a master."

"That's an interesting choice of teachers," Suren volunteered.

"Why?"

"He's Greco's Ligerian bastard."

13

The king and Claudine and Tuli returned to the royal suite directly, preoccupied, silent. At Claudine's outer door, where they paused, the king invited them into his salon for cocktails. Claudine demurred: "Work to do in my room—through dinner, which will be sandwiches."

"Nothing so austere for me," returned the king. "I shall dine formally at the captain's table. But after dinner?"

"I have that date," Claudine reminded.

"True," sighed the king, bowing slightly. "What time?"

"2130 hours, at the theater."

"Then perhaps would you and Chief Tuli favor me by tippling my cocktails at 2030 hours?"

In Claudine's room, Tuli said grimly: "Not much time left, Lieutenant."

Having shuddered ritually at her action-inverted wristwatch, Claudine checked her cutichron and responded: "1800 hours. We have, it appears, between sixteen and twenty hours before the thing goes radiant—or establishes that it won't go radiant without more acceleration. And if we then accelerate, it will go radiant. And if we don't accelerate—two years to Ligeria, with a little more than a one-year supply of water on half-rations."

"To be precise," Tuli added, "when we approach Ligeria, in order to brake for landing, we will have to accelerate."

"So then, when we long-dead zombies activate the landing acceleration, we go stellar. I think I prefer eighteen hours."

"I agree," said Tuli practically, "because Ligeria right now doesn't look so good."

"Since you agree, it is time to tell you about *Sodim e Gomorrh.*"

Producing the little band, Claudine told Tuli all about it. Tuli's response was blank. "Nothing, Lieutenant. But I will check it."

"We have, at best, eighteen hours—since after we nail the guy, we have to get him to change things."

"I will check it fast."

"I don't know how, since you have to guard the king tonight."

"I do?"

"Starting at 2100 hours. Until I don't know when."

"Yeoman Gringle is good at this stuff. May I call him now?"

Time was wasted while he got there—but not much. Claudine gave him the picture, and she added: "Your big problem is to avoid letting it be known that I am the one who wants this information. If you have a drinking-gambling buddy on the crew, get *him* to find out for you—unless he knows already. And try to get the band back from him, I might need it for evidence."

"I have," said the yeoman, "a totally suitable drinking-gambling buddy."

En route to the place where his drinking-gambling buddy would probably be, the yeoman passed the open door of a classroom where interested passengers were being coached in the dominant Ligerian language. The emerging sounds were interesting, and he paused by the door.

107

"—Already dinnertime," the teacher was saying. "My, *doesn't* time fly when things are intriguing? We must stop now—but first, shall we test what we have learned?"

There was a mass class sound: "MMMMmmm."

"Let us then," cooed the female teacher, "consider four key sentences. All answer in Ligerian unison. *The girl is pretty.*"

"Vola me belisand."

"The paper is white."

"Glostre ma sodim."

"The money is gold."

"Palaz ma gomorrh."

"The man is ugly."

"Hego mo zizin."

"Very good, class. Shall we break up for dinner?"

The yeoman got away from the door before he could be crushed by the rush. His buddy Joe was unquestionably at the crew bar. He was glad he didn't have to communicate his mission in Ligerian.

The biography of Captain Schwarz fascinated Claudine, although Tuli found it rather disreputable for a ranking officer. "Why?" Claudine demanded. "Too flashy," Tuli sniffed. Actually, nothing was out of line at all. That was the trouble: absolutely no hint of a potential enemy—although many of his exploits suggested that he might have formed a great many actual enemies.

Claudine was looking particularly for a link with Greco —the elder, that is: not Doré, but Old Fire-Eyes. One was there, but it was tenuous and indirect: Tuli had to point it out. Fourteen years before, young Lieutenant-Commander Schwarz had commanded a shore party which quelled a disturbance on Maruvia. "I checked," said Tuli, "and it was Greco who manufactured the disturbance, although he isn't identified here." Claudine commented that Mashti was a Maruvian—conceivably he might have conceived animosity toward Schwarz on the same occasion—but of course it was unlikely: the disturbance had not even occurred on a sapsucking conti-

108

nent; and had Mashti been present, probably it would have been as a junior officer in the Schwarz party.

They perused the report several times, however, if only for entertainment. It picked up the career of Schwarz when he entered the Galactic Space Navy at the age of twenty. After serving in two interplanetary wars (gallantly!), he had risen to the rank of lieutenant-commander. The little action on Maruvia had been his last as a naval officer: soon afterward he had joined the Merchant Astcrine on an unrefusable bid from the company that owned the *Eiland of Ligeria;* and one year later, he had become first officer of the *Eiland,* with the expectation—realized—of succeeding her retiring captain in command.

The biographical material was drawn from a number of sources, including society pages and gossip columns. A number of affairs were mentioned—of the heart, and of the blood. The most pleasing aspect of this entertainment was the absence of bad taste: Schwarz had had grace: even when he was twice seriously wounded in combat, neither of the wounds was in bad taste. His hobbies, it appeared, were beautiful married women, good cigars, old timepieces, and old magic. His annual leave-disappearances were noted by several columnists: it was variously rumored that he was secretly a prince or a narcotics king or a star ballet dancer on this, that, or another planet.

"How could a man like that be kept on as captain of the *Eiland of Ligeria?*" fumed Tuli.

"How could they let him go?" Claudine countered. "But I am just becoming aware of a curious hiatus in this material—his first twenty years. We don't know a thing about his youth, not even where he was born."

"We have the most recent quarter-century," Tuli reminded her, "and it's unlikely that anything earlier was involved in his killing. As for his birthplace—with that name, and the many times he used to slip into German —where *would* he be born?"

"Ligeria, maybe. Most of this crew was."

"You have a hunch about that?"

"What I have a hunch about is that something in his life earlier than the past quarter-century was indirectly involved in his death."

"Just a hunch?"

"Just a hunch. Nothing more."

"I've learned to respect your hunches," declared the chief, "but as of now I go along with your recent reasoning. Schwarz wasn't killed because he was Schwarz, only because he was captain. His killing and Swainson's murder were merely incidental to the murder of this ship. The most likely suspect is Greco, who likely killed the two captains one after another as religious dramatics, maybe using his, ah, illegitimate son Doré to do the work. The second most likely is Mashti, who killed them to get command; the third is Suren, who killed them because they knew how to bypass the DM and save the ship. I don't see anything for us in this Schwarz dossier, Lieutenant."

"That's your longest speech in a week. Somehow I feel that you disapprove of Schwarz—"

"Are you dead set on this, ah, meeting with Doré?"

"This date tonight? Of course."

"And you won't take me along."

"Tuli! But what would my date think?"

The door opened slightly, and the king announced: "Cocktail time, fuzz."

Claudine entered the salon, followed by the chief. The king was dressed loungey, on his feet, holding a highball. "Sit down, ladies," he invited. "May I pour you something?"

"Zac on the rocks," Claudine specified.

"Nothing, thank you," demurred Chief Tuli with total primness. Her hands were folded in her lap. Her suit was gray tweed, her skirt long enough so that by plucking at it she could get it definitely below the knee. (Claudine wore a yellow blouse—no coat—and a tan skirt that she didn't bother to pluck.)

The king accorded Tuli what Claudine amusedly recognized as the practiced male lightning-glance which appraises fully without seeming to stare. He nodded and went

110

to make zac on the rocks and water on the rocks. Returning, he handed Claudine her zac, and then bowed before the chief, offering her the water. She took it with a strained smile on the rocks and sipped.

Now the king sat, looking at Claudine with an eyebrow up.

"I need to remind you, sir," said Claudine, "that I am going to be away from you, possibly all night, and the chief here will take my place. You will be adequately covered. She has a weapon, but she can kill with her bare hands. Also we have yeomen in the corridor."

He returned courteously," looking at Tuli: "In the chief's hands I feel entirely safe."

Tuli acknowledged crisply: "Your Majesty, you may."

"And that is more than I can say for the hands of Lieutenant St. Cyr."

Claudine grinned, coloring; Tuli frosted. Wiping off her own grin, Claudine soberly changed the subject: "I've been looking for a chance to say how sorry I am about the developments on Ligeria. Excuse me, I have to tell Tuli everything connected with our assignment—but she won't talk, not even to our own people."

Actually the king's eyes twinkled. "Thank you for not reminding me how beloved I thought I was. Really, I had no idea that matters had progressed this far. I should like to regain the throne just long enough to decapitate my chief of intelligence—except that my enemies have probably beaten me to it."

"Have you plans yet, sir?"

He shook his head slowly. "I am planning, but I have not formed them. I am in idaradio contact with Galactic, but I can't get through to Ligeria. This is one time when I don't mind loafing along in freefall, DM or no DM. By the way—is it permitted for me to know *why* my lieutenant may be absent all night?"

"You know that I will be with Doré."

"Yes, and I vaguely understand why; but—all night?"

"If necessary," Claudine responded, not coloring.

"Before explanations begin," he interrupted, looking at the chief, "there is another thing that I have been curious

111

about. Miss Tuli was introduced me to me as Chief Detective's Mate U. Tuli. To be blunt—what is the U. for?"

Uncomfortable silence. Claudine told Tuli: "Chief, if this is privileged information, the king will understand." Turning to glare at the king, she thundered: "WON'T YOU!"

"Well, sure," he responded mildly. "Forget it."

"Ultima," said Tuli.

"I beg your pardon?"

Chief Tuli was frozen like the north wind. "The U. stands for Ultima."

"And that," declared Claudine, "is privileged information."

"I will only ask," murmured the king, "whether you have any younger siblings."

"Yes. Five."

Silence.

Turning to Claudine, he queried: "Is it time now to explain why all night? Not that you have to."

Claudine, examining her fingernails, told him: "I do not say that this date will be all business; but insofar as it is business, and that is plenty, you should thoroughly understand what I am after. It is *your* captains who have been murdered and *your* ship's passengers who are in danger of space-death."

"And *my* life, among the others, that is at stake." He started to work on a cigar.

"You undoubtedly gathered, from our discussion in the Communications Cabin this afternoon, that flipping seems to have been involved in all three crimes: the lethal catabolium was created by changing the spin on inner-orbit electrons—"

"That's a pretty high order of flipping."

"I imagine. And the hearts of Captain Schwarz and Commander Swainson were turned inside-out and then righted again."

"How do you flip-flop a heart without breaking it loose from its pipes?"

"That was Suren's question."

"Has it been answered?"

112

"No."

"Go on."

"So I need two things from young Doré. In the first place, he is the best flipper I know about, and the only one I know about on this ship; from him I need an intensive course in the technique. Second, Greco is the prime suspect; and since Doré turns out to be Greco's son, he just might also turn-out to be Greco's tool. So getting all this—instruction from him just may take all night."

Courteously the king awaited the next thing that she would say.

Claudine stood, brows level. "I only want to be sure," she asserted icily, "that you will make no attempt to draw any inferences that are unrelated to the duty that I have to perform."

"My inferences," he stated, "are my own business. But I will not communicate them, and they will not affect my attitudes."

They gazed at each other.

She nodded once, and left—not slamming the door, but shutting it quite definitely.

Then, just for an instant, she put an ear against the door.

He was saying to Chief Tuli: "Do you think you can handle another shot of water?"

Part Three

THE GREAT DORÉ

14

She met him backstage, just before showtime. She was ushered into his tiny dressing room; he swung around and leaped to his feet with a delighted smile and seized both her hands. "You," he exclaimed, "are a dreamboat!" Claudine let out head-back laughter: she was charmed, he was charming, it was no line at all, it was just good.

They talked with animation for half an hour, into the start of the show, comparing notes on origins, interests (he liked freefall handball and scuba and was an amateur of antique stagemagic), childhoods (his had been jungle-edge grubby). Then apologetically he interrupted, and took her out of his room and up a narrow open-metal stairway and sat her on a stool poised precariously on a high, slender stage-overlook, suggesting: "See if you can spot any mirrors!" and left her to watch the nudie ballet while he went below to make last-minute preparations for his own act.

She watched nothing; she had gone all blue inside. He *was* the handsomest guy she had ever met—long-faced, big-eyed, long-nosed, wide-mouthed, lithe, easily smiling; his complexion was perfectly clear—more of a pale yellow than the typical range from chrome-yellow to yellow-brown of the golden Ligerians. But beyond this, he was a *nice* guy. So she was about to trick this handsome nice guy into a confession of murder and ship-sabotage. Never mind how professionally he'd brought it off, if he had: he'd done it, if he had. Never mind if he was a tool for his father, Paranoid Mastermind Greco: still he'd

117

done it, and he was old enough to know better. So what was Claudine? a bitch using her sex to milk him of knowledge and maybe a confession. . . .

Heigh-ho, she sighed: police work! You couldn't present evidence obtained with bugs or lie detectors or mental telepathy or unrestricted hypnosis, but sex you could use. It had been challenged way back in 2034—the Earthworld Court had upheld this kind of evidence on the ground that an insane defendant would get off anyhow while a sane one was supposed to watch out for women on principle—and the courts today in their historic archaism were clinging to this feudal procedure. . . .

Materializing beside her on the backstage platform, he cried: "Here we go, Claudine! Watch!" And he simply stepped off into space, his momentum carrying him languidly forward about three meters, and hung there while the curtain opened and the applause thundered, and then descended on a trajectory and went into his impossible act.

With professional expertise she scrutinized his act again in all its intricate transpository detail, and could find no flaw, only new marvels. Fascinating how this essentially naive boy, once on stage, fell into a *suavité* that King Zhavàr might envy!

And when it was done, she half-hoped that he would fly back up to her aerie; but instead he ran up the stair like flying, and seized her hands again, and wanted breathlessly to know whether she had liked it from up here.

Then he brought her down, and sat her on a stool outside his cubicle while he dressed, and called her in when he was half-decent, and chattered while he fixed the rest of himself. Whirling, he sat back on his dressing table, leaning down over her as she crouched delighted in a chair against the far wall six feet away. "I've arranged supper in my room," he told her. "What do you think—is it all right?"

Her smile of clear pleasure wanted to come; and she told the smile it was all right, it was part of the act as

118

well as being genuine; and the smile came, and she said one throaty word: "Lovely!"

It sort of stunned him, his answering smile was wan, he started to say something, abruptly he turned back to his mirror and adjusted his necktie. Then he turned again, all eager boy again, and cried, "Come on!" and seized her hand and drew her out to the stage door and on to Frolic Street.

And there were the sidewalk café and the Ligerian mountebanks (one fewer than before) and the music museum and the go-go theater and the sidewalk café and the overhead stars and all the people here below (below?) . . .

And the shop of the watchmaker, with its funny cigar-counter out front, framed with white and gold like blond zebrawood. . . .

At first it seemed that he was leading her to this shop. He did pause in front of it: the shop was closed, and he peered through the glass of the door into its depths. He shrugged: "In his workshop, likely. Doesn't matter—we don't want to see him now!" Leading her past the shop into a little narrow old alley, he took her through a rickety doorway (on a *starship?*) and up a flight of stairs (which should have been rickety but instead was metallic-firm) and down a narrow short corridor. He palmed a door-eye, and the door disappeared, and he led her in, and the door reappeared, immuring them.

She was in his tiny apartment, alone with him. It was just after 2300 hours. A great deal of night was ahead of her.

15

Instead of vichyssoise and beef Stroganoff and three wines, he served grilled ham and scrambled eggs and *vin ordinaire*. It was marvelous. They talked the hell out of the supper.

Toward the end, Claudine—without noticeably changing attitude—commanded herself to get down to business. Her idea of business in this context, though, was not to ask "Where were you on the night of X-Y?" but instead to ask, "You mean *all* of us have trouble with our parents?"

Forking-in the last bit of ham, he told her enthusiastically: "With yours you should have had my trouble. Was *your* father a crowd-shouting do-gooder who surreptitiously dropped in on your mother when he happened to be in her part of the jungle?"

"Mine," Claudine reminisced, "was a crowd-looting do-badder, but otherwise the similarity is noteworthy."

"So you revolted and went straight."

"Right."

"Became a cop, even. A wowser-straighter." His grin was a coal scuttle, he slopped wine over his glass-rim.

"Right. And the best little cop you ever did see."

He went moody. "Now why didn't I revolt and go bad?"

"I'm surprised you didn't. I thought it was mostly the boys who threw the toughest adolescent rebellions."

He had gone glum. "But my pop is a hypnotist."

"Oh?" It was the pay-dirt trail. For some reason, thought, she wasn't caring for it.

He was back up to just moody, now—he shifted

120

moods liquidly like a colorama. "Pop would show up once or twice a year, drive Mom and me nuts for a few weeks, then leave her to shift for herself with me and three other bastards, two of them his. Mom just took it and got anemic, she died when I was about eight. So I took charge, and begged and stole and so on, keeping us going. Pop came back and found us; he was grief-stricken, sternly so; but he didn't let himself grieve, instead he told himself that it must have been something he'd done wrong, so he upped his chin and drove into his religious act all the stronger. He dumped off my two little sisters and brother with a missionary orphanage, not letting on they were his; and he took me with him on his travels."

"How did he keep you from spilling the beans?" There was no doubt that Doré was talking about Greco.

"Hypnosis. He had me good by then, he'd been training me to respond to him from infancy. He had a three-planet circuit, mostly bumming his way between on tramp freighters: and every time I tried to louse up his preacher hypocrisy by telling somebody he was my pop, my throat nearly turned inside-out. I had to run away, I *had* to."

"How old were you then?" She was infinitely solicitous.

"Thirteen."

"I bet you've felt guilty ever since."

Shaking his head, he met her eyes. "I haven't felt anything about that. I just haven't felt."

It was in the pattern. "So you found a career. Flipping."

He smiled tight. "How about that! Where I ran away, it was on Ligeria, not far from the old thatched homestead. I found hiding-sanctuary in the home of an old wise man I knew—like what they call a *guru* in your India—and he taught me how to flip. Nothing like what you saw me do on the stage—just easy standard stuff, like throwing oneself into a deathlike suspense of animation, or transposing a couple of grapes. Finally he said I didn't have the sanctimony to be a *guru,* I should make a secular career out of flipping, and—*voici!* Hey, how about the French, Claudine?"

121

"Très bien, Monsieur Doré!"

"Name's Jim. Well, natively it's Lizhin, but it translates Jim."

"Jim."

"Claudine."

Mutually engrossed pause.

He jumped to his feet. "Here, I'll clear off the dishes. More wine?" The dishes went into a wall disposal, and he poured and sat, leaning eagerly toward her across the little table. "Let's talk about you."

She repressed a desire to do just that: their childhoods had been intimately alike: city jungle and country jungle were transposable. "Not now," she begged. "Keep going —you've had a marvelous life, Jim! How did you get to be good in the act?"

He spread hands. "Let's see. Well, I knocked around in little backwoods demonstrations for a few years, collecting what you'd call rupees and getting better and better. I had the feel of it, you see, and I would go off in the jungle and experiment with stuff, and when I could do something reliably well, I'd put it into my act. Then when I was nineteen, I got a chance to work my way across the ocean to Vanya—that's the main continent on Ligeria, mostly white. I got bookings, and for about a year I toured the sticks in Vanya.

"A year later, my act was spotted by a white Ligerian who had a—well, a *private* show. For some reason he only gave it one weekend each year, in Vanya's summer which corresponds to Earth's northern wintertime. He picked me up as his assistant. He was the greatest master of ultra-complex flipping that I have ever seen—no golden *guru* can come within parsecs of him! Every summer he would pick me up wherever I was, and tutor me intensively for a week, and then we'd give our weekend show, and then he'd tutor me for another week, and then chase me away. Each season, when he released me to go it alone, I was better, stronger, had more scope. The third season, he made me his junior partner in the act. He called himself the Great Blanchet, mainly because he was about as white as a Ligerian comes, and French is a sign

122

of elegance in Vanya. Well: so because I am golden, it amused him to call me the Great Doré—"

"What *had* you been calling yourself?" She wanted to go on and ask: "The Great Greco?" but she didn't.

"The Mystery Man," he grinned. "Corny, no? The Great Doré is parsecs better. So our act became known as Blanchet and Doré—as much as to say, White and Gold, the planetary colors of Ligeria."

"Appropriate." Something in the back of her mind was making small fuzzy noises.

"Wasn't it? Blanchet was *brilliant!* You can see how I gradually came to regard him as my real father."

"So how did you suddenly get a star act aboard the *Eiland?*"

"*His* influence. Blanchet."

Claudine was confused. "How?"

He frowned. "This I can't tell even you. I promised."

"Okay—but I'm fascinated by this private showing—one weekend every summer. Where was it?"

"In the palace."

"In what palace?" Then her eyes widened: "The palace of the King of Ligeria?"

He smiled proudly: "Just there." His eyes went reminiscent: "When I signed aboard the *Eiland,* it rather shocked *Drop Dead!*, they knew me only as a Ligerian bushwhacker. But it was in the palace that I got to be good—and of course, Blanchet knew it."

In Claudine's mind was colorfully evolving the preposterous fantasy that King Zhavàr might turn out to be the master flipper who pleasured himself for one weekend each year with private showings in his palace, who had adopted young Jim as his protégé: had he not declared keen special interest in Doré? and who else would both know about obscure Doré and have enough influence to get him aboard the *Eiland* as a headliner? If the king could be coaxed into admitting this, he could be invaluable in helping to identify the criminal and save his own ship. . . .

"Tell me this much," she wheedled. "Is Blanchet aboard the *Eiland* this voyage?"

123

Jim went stubborn. "This I cannot tell you," Oddly, small tears appeared.

So then it *was* the king—maybe; for if the Great Blanchet were *not* aboard, it would have done no harm for Jim to say so. Well: perhaps already the king was instructing himself to admit to her his annual royal peccadillo, realizing that he could save the ship if the criminal were not caught or, caught, could not be persuaded to act. If saving were possible, that is.

If the king were Blanchet . . . And yet, who else? And just in case he should deny it, a quick private idaradio exchange with Galactic should settle it: they *must* have more on him beyond the *Who's Who* extract!

Fascinating gay-grave father figure whose personality was veils beyond veils. And now *this* unbelievable-believable facet . . .

16

"What do you think of my act, Claudine?" It was a gay almost-immediate change of subject after his refusal to say whether Blanchet was aboard.

Thinking all the time, she responded: "Terrific, Jim! Do you think your father would be proud?"

He went confidential, leaning farther forward. "This is just between us, but—what would you say if I told you that my father *is* aboard?"

She directed herself to lean backward with astonishment. "No!" In her work there were ethical quandaries: for instance, if you were questioning a suspect, and he claimed your confidence in a revelation pertinent to the business, what did you do? In this case, however, she had already known about the Greco-Doré relationship: she

124

could reveal it without a breach of confidence, although it might be hard to convince Jim of this. You had to follow your conscience and expect to be castigated.

His eyes held her. "Claudine—my father is Greco! Old Fire-Eyes!"

She grabbed for a reply. "Is *he* your father?"

His face went mocking-sorrowful. "You saw him perform last night. I hope you won't hold it against me."

"Of course not." Was that the right answer?

"No, he wouldn't be proud of my shenanigans! I was better tonight, knowing that he was in jail."

Up went her eyebrows. "But he wasn't in jail yesterday afternoon—and you were terrific *then!"*

Down went his. "I didn't know he was aboard, until last night."

Either it was a plain lie, or something was wacky here. He *had* to be Greco's instrument to contaminate the DM —and this had occurred before the show she'd seen. Decidedly he was the nicest naive-type liar she'd ever met. Leaning forward, she pressed: "Jim—*why* do you still let your father intimidate you?"

He went serious. "He hypnotizes me."

It jolted her into a cold confrontation with lethal ugliness. She managed to inquire mildly: "Still?"

"He must have lowered my resistance in childhood so completely that it set forever. One look and he has me."

"What does he make you do?"

"Nothing. At least—nothing as far as I know. He probably tells me to forget everything before he brings me out of it. I just know I've been hypnotized. One look, and I like him: it *must* be hypnosis."

Claudine was frowning into her wine. He demanded: "What's the matter?"

She wanted to follow up this hypnosis thing, but first she had to bring in another rather complicated precinct. Shaking her head, she swiftly improvised: "Nothing. I've gone intellectual, is all. I got thinking about your show technique."

"Did you spot something sloppy?"

Up came her head, and her mouth was half-happy. "Heck no! I just go wondering how you do it."

He spread hands, smiling with a kind of wonder. "Dunno. I just do."

"F'rinstance, you dunno how you hang in the air at the start and slowly descend to the stage?"

"Oh, that!" he grinned. "That's the only fake in my show. You won't tell?"

"Natch not." She meant it: no evident courtroom application.

"That's just antigrav."

"On *you?* but in your tights there are no unusual bulges—"

"No no. From under the *floor!* Special installation."

"Oh." She looked rueful; probably every *man* in the audience assumed this. "But you say the rest is—"

"The rest is honest. Straightforward flipping."

"And this means, psychokinetics—moving stuff around by force of mind."

"That's right. You look at me, you gather it doesn't take much mind."

"I want to question you, Jim. I happen to be a psychologist." The partial self-revelation irrationally relieved her of guilt totally, and she knew that it was phony relief.

"Good for you!" he exclaimed. "I knew you couldn't just be a cop!"

Again she was jolted—she'd forgotten that he knew. So then, anyhow, *nothing* was under the table—or practically nothing. Her phony relief became real. She said: "Damn you, sir."

"For which insult?"

"Damn you again, sir!"

They got laughing. Bringing himself around, he laid a hand on her hand on the table and assured her: "Fire away. I never mind questions I can't answer."

Her hand rested comfortably under his. She demanded: "How do you do it?"

He went serious. "I just do. I told you I study."

"What I mean—tell me what happens in your brain."

He spread hands, releasing hers. "I haven't the fog-

126

giest. I just—*will* for it to happen, and it *does*. Like walking and talking."

She ventured: "I've studied it too, a little—but objectively, I can't do it myself. But I could tell you a little about what happens where, in your brain. Would that help you get to be even better?"

He frowned, shaking his head slowly. "I'd rather not know. It would be like the centipede who got along fine until somebody asked him about the order of his footwork."

She nodded. "I see what you mean. All right. But still, Jim—tell me in your own words: how do you do it?"

He looked up. "Are you asking me as a psychologist, Cop?"

She let herself smile faintly. "I'm asking you as a pro, Pro."

He grinned broad. "All right. You're asking me as Claudine, Jim."

She smiled in whole spontaneity. "Exactly."

He went serious: it was the intellectual mood. "I went through quite a course of training, Claudine. There are several progressive steps to this. Do you want to get systematic?"

She went grave, matching the mood. "I'm not unused to it."

"Good. More wine?"

"Bitte."

For some reason, he winced at the *bitte;* but he said "Good" and went to get it.

17

"Mind if I pull up my chair beside you?" he queried, pulling up his chair beside her.

"Not at all, but I'm disappointed that you used your hands."

"Sometimes I just get careless. I am now going into it. Ready?"

"Shoot."

"Well, Flipping: Short Course in. First of all, there's *simple transposition.* That's when, like, I transpose vests between two people."

"That's simple?"

"Almost as easy as transposing a couple of grapes. Everybody who can do any of this stuff can do that."

"All right, I've seen you do it. What's tougher?"

"Of course, the multiple inter-vest ballet routine I do isn't easy—"

"You make it look easy."

"That's the hardest part."

She grinned. "I know. I'm needling. You're terrific, Jim." Her inward eyebrow twitched—she noticed that she really and warmly meant it: he *was!*

"Shucks!" he grinned back—they were both being fatuous, and loving it. "So you want to know what's tougher? Just a minute—" Rising, he swung over to a wall, palmed open a drawer, and produced a pair of heavy leather gloves. Laying one on the table, he said: "Watch." The glove lay motionless—and then she realized that it was now inside-out, although it hadn't been before.

"Simple inversion," he announced. "That's the next tougher thing."

"Why is it tougher?"

"I don't know. It is."

"You still don't want me to tell you how I think you do it?"

He shook his head positively. "Don't break the spell—I'm doing fine in my ignorance. Now the next thing that duffers learn to do—"

"Duffers?"

"So far I am only showing you stuff that most any experienced flipper can learn to do if he stays at it. And the next thing at this same level is *mirror-inversion*. Watch the glove." Again it did not move, but suddenly it was right-side-out again.

"You mean—just putting it back the way it was?"

"No. More. Look at it carefully."

She caught on. "Before, it was a right glove. Now it's a left glove."

"Exactly. Neat?"

"It ain't easy."

"You realize that I used this principle too, in my act?"

"I sure do," she glowed, watching him fondly. (Well, *flut!* do I have to *hate* a suspect? Besides, look how nicely he's coming out with all this. . . .)

They were seated now at the same side of the table. Sitting sidewise, hands folded between his knees, he leaned toward her. "But you realize I didn't do anything *more* difficult—except for the complexity and neatness?"

"You didn't?"

"No ma'am! That's as far as I went. Because the next step is a major leap across a threshold, like when an atom moves out one orbit; and when you get to that next step, you don't do it in time to music in front of a lot of spectators!"

She laid a hand on his folded hands, intensely interested. "So what is the next step?"

"*Structural* inversion."

"Like?"

"Like when the inner surface of a ball becomes its outer surface—and *vice versa*."

129

The trail was heating up. Claudine blinked: "Can you do *that?*"

"Yep."

"How? Without splitting the ball, I mean?" Claudine was reflecting that this would be a rough analogy with inverting a human heart—disregarding, that is, the complication of not snapping off the pipes.

"I don't know how, I told you."

"You aren't being petulant?"

"No, really, it isn't that. I just—maybe it didn't come through to you—"

"Yes, it did," she told him, "and I think you may be right—I've seen too many people ruined by reading books on psychology. But that isn't what I mean, this time. I'm not asking you what happens in your brain—I'm asking what happens to the ball."

"Oh. That. Well, it depends, you see, on how good the flipper is. Because it depends on how well he can envision the inward structure of the ball—or whatever the object may be."

"So what structure does a ball have, except roundness and hollowness?"

"The skin of a hollow ball has appreciable thickness—maybe two or three or five millimeters. And the outside surface is larger than the inside surface. When you invert the ball, what you are really doing is a sophisticated form of a point-for-point transposition: the large outside becomes the small inside, the small inside becomes the large outside, the in-between in between. So the inside, becoming suddenly larger, has to spread; while the outside, going inward and becoming suddenly smaller, has either to compress or to buckle. In order to pull off this kind of inversion successfully, you have to mentally provide for these changes before you act. I really did the same thing with the glove; but since the glove is soft and its skin-thickness isn't great, I was able to neglect the preplanning. Here, I have some practice balls: let me show you."

He brought out four of them and set them on the table. The phone chimed. "Excuse me," he said; "hell of a time to call—" While he was at the wall phone, she examined

130

the balls, only partially alert to him: all four of them were golden. She heard him disconnect after several "Hellos," and he returned and sat beside her: "Nobody at all at the other end—must have called the wrong number, realized it, must have disconnected before I answered. Okay: the balls. The outside is gold, the inside white. Now, with this first one, I will merely do a simple inversion as I did with the glove, not thinking about the size problems that I mentioned. Watch."

He regarded the ball fixedly. It exploded with a pop, three or four fragments flew, the bulk of it crouched ruined.

"That in itself," said Claudine, "is spectacular."

"Now," he told her intently, "I have moved forward a bit in the art. To prevent that explosion from happening, I am mentally arranging for systematic splits to occur in the thickness of the ball. . . . Here, you won't grasp that too clearly if you are thinking of a solid figure: let me first show you how it works with a ring." From the junk drawer he brought out a flat ring about three centimeters in diameter outside, its hollow two centimeters inside. Holding it up, he urged: "Watch this." Abruptly all around the ring appeared a system of wedge-shaped splits, wide agape outside, coming down to V-closures inside, while the inside surface appeared irregularly buckled. "I inverted this," he told her. "Do you see what happened?"

She tried: "You mentally made cuts at regular intervals from the inside to just short of the outside surface. Then, when you inverted the ring, the insided-outside just buckled, while the outsided-inside spread open."

"You *are* sharp!" he warmed her by saying. "Now, it would be pretty hard to express just what analogously will happen to the ball—except that it will be the same sort of thing, only in three dimensions instead of two. Watch."

The second gold ball all at once became white, but otherwise it seemed normal. He handed it to her, with a magnifying glass: the outside surface was intricately marked with tiny fissures. He showed her, for comparison, the third ball which had not been treated: even under the glass, its surface was only somewhat porous.

She mused: "If you could show me the inside of this inverted ball, it would be buckled."

"Right."

"What happens if you put it back again?"

Under her fingers the ball seemed to writhe. Inadvertently she dropped it; it bounced, golden again; laughing, he caught it and handed it back to her. She studied it with the glass. "Looks normal."

Taking it, he sliced it in two with a knife and handed it back. "Examine the cross-section."

"Yes. I can see the cuts."

She paused. She mused: "Like tiny *strain-lines*."

"I hadn't thought of that. You're right. But they are cuts, squeezed tight-closed by the restored structure of the ball."

In a way, it was almost sickening, how he was practically confessing the murders; but she made herself stay ebullient. She didn't ask him how he managed simultaneously to envision and create all those cuts—she knew the principle involved, and he didn't want to: once the mind generalizes a structure, and adds a general demand that it be serially replicated, the computer-brain, if trained, takes care of it automatically. Instead, she commented: "There are two more balls."

"The next step up in skill," said Jim thoughtfully, "would be theoretically to condense the molecules on the outside while spreading apart the molecules on the inside; and then one would get a completely uncut, instrained inversion. However, molecular relationships in a solid are tremendously rigid, and that is almost impossible to do. Paradoxically, it is easier to alter intra-atomic relationships."

"That's a pretty high order of mentation, Jim."

"When you catch on to *how,* it works all right. You don't have to treat each atom separately—you don't even have to treat each *kind* of atom separately. An atom maintains its size and structure by maintaining a balance of thrust-and-draw as between its electrons and its nucleus. So all I have to do is arrange that draw will exceed thrust in the atoms of the outer surface, and that thrust will exceed draw in the atoms of the inner surface, and proportionately in between. Then I invert—and no optical microscope can reveal any abnormality."

"As easy as *that?*" She was aware that by revealing his knowledge of intra-atomic flipping, he had come exceedingly close to saying that he had the ability to do what had been done to the DM-component. Not quite, however; for precisely what had been done there was to change electronic spin, which was a different proposition.

"Well," Doré admitted, "there is one problem. When I change these balances, the effects develop almost instantaneously, so I have to invert instantaneously. If I drag for a fraction of a second—watch that third ball."

With a pop it disappeared.

She blinked.

He demanded: "Tell me what happened."

She said: "The atomic disruptions tore apart the molecular patterns: all atoms were freed from each other, and they are all swarming away into the atmosphere."

He laid a hand on her wrist, looking into her eyes. "You know so *much?*"

She returned his gaze steadily, deliciously.

He murmured: "I could teach you—oh, *all* these things!"

She continued to gaze at him—caught herself—gulped, and inquired: "How about the fourth ball?"

He held her eyes and her wrist a moment longer; then he turned his attention to the ball. "With the third ball," he said low, "I showed you how to do the atomic thing wrong; with this one, I will do it right. First I am going to examine the ball carefully, without doing anything to it, mainly to get my attention focused on the problem. Then I will close my eyes in order to get the intra-atomic arrangements mentally set. When I am sure, I will open my eyes and do all of it at once."

She held her breath.

Without looking away from the golden ball, he said quietly: "This will take a little time. So breathe."

She giggled once, then watched, breathing shallowly.

He closed his eyes. He kept his head rigid, so that his closed eyes were still aimed at the ball.

His eyes came open.

Calmly the ball became white.

She let out breath: *"Ahhhh!"*

He turned to her, smiling shyly, spreading hands.

Her honest admiration dwelt upon him. She could love him. And it wasn't mere erotics that she felt. He was naive. He was brilliant. He was shy. He was *real*.

He gazed at her.

She gazed at him.

Clearing her throat, she suggested unevenly: "Is that the best that you can do?"

His mouth-corners quirked upward. "It happens to be the best that *I* can do—*yet*. But I am working on the next step."

The constriction in her stomach and chest signaled her inward rebellion against this detective work. Nevertheless she led him along: "Are you going to tell a guy what it is?"

"You need more wine."

"Well, yes."

He arose to get it. "I've just been showing you the simplest kind of structural inversion," he tossed over his shoulder. "Even the snazzy atomic kind is only the hardest of the simplest, and it is very superficial atomic work. And yet even that," he went on, coming with the wine, uncorking, "is a major threshold leap above simple inversion. Actually there are"—pouring—"three levels of structural inversion: *hollow* structural inversion—what I just showed you—" He paused, corking. "If you're so damned smart, *guess* what the next two are."

"The next would be *solid* structural inversion."

"Deep. And?"

"Well . . . Let's say, two kinds of solid structural inversion: the *spherical* kind, and the more difficult *angular or irregular* kind."

He was setting down the bottle on a side table as she

134

said it. He just stayed there, back to her, hand on the bottleneck. He said softly: "May the great bottle-fly god of the Ligerian equator sting my bottle!"

She gasped with pleasure. "Was I—*right?*"

He swung, came up behind her, squeezed her shoulders —she looking back and up. "What you said is what it is."

Her soft grin was lip-closed, with the lower lip out a bit; her eyes squinted as she syrup-responded, "Aw, shucks."

His grin flared wide, and he gave her shoulders one big squeeze, then released them as though they'd shocked him and came around to sit beside her again and peer into her face. "You knew before? No, you didn't! You just got, like they say, logical."

She went sober. "Natch. I'm a cop." Nobody could say she hadn't reminded him.

Artlessly he assured her: "You don't have to be a cop. You're good enough to be anything."

Tartly she responded: "Copping ain't so easy, either."

Pause, mutually engrossed.

She said sultry: "You really can't do solid yet?"

He just shook his head, looking at her.

A small voice deep inside her murmured: "Lovely liar!" What she said was: "Know anything about it?"

He nodded vaguely.

"Know anybody who does it?"

He cleared his throat and said: "I told you my master Blanchet could do anything. He told me. He showed me. But we split up before I could really begin work at that level."

"How good *was* Blanchet?" The king, maybe? Nawww . . .

"Best in the galaxy." Impulsively he seized her forearm. "Claudine, you know what he could do? He could invert the head of a golf stick, and revert it—without even snapping it off the stick!"

Her eyes closed. The hearts—without snapping pipes . . . The relevancy here was that a heart would require an interblend of hollow and solid inversion. *Sure* Jim could do it; play it along, though . . . "Jim—imagine

135

something like that with a ball-type hollow inversion. Suppose the ball faired-off into something like a golf stick—"

His forehead puckered. "Give me an honest f'rinstance."

She puckered too—she couldn't mention a heart with arteries. "I can't think of one."

He ventured: "Maybe a ball-reactor at the end of a shaft?"

"Maybe."

"How big?"

"Does it matter?"

"Its mass matters, but not its magnitude. Anything from a grape to a planet—a light planet, that is. You just have to be at enough distance to comprise it all within your visual field. Telepsychic phenomena sneer at distance."

"That's a good sentence there." But—mass mattered?

"I know. I've been three years reworking it."

"Well—can you?"

"Can I what?"

"Invert the ball-reactor without snapping it off the shaft?"

"Nope. But Blanchet could."

"How?"

"I don't want to—"

"Not how in his brain—how with the reactor."

"Oh. He said he just figured an arbitrary plane of cleavage, fixed three binding counterpoints on the two sides of the plane, and held them while he flipped. When he flipped back, molecular adhesion patterns restored themselves—and there you were."

"Mm-*hm!* Sounds easy."

"It isn't. I can't."

Overinsisting, Jim? Yet why would you reveal to me that you know how? She switched it: "Get back to spherical solids then. How would Blanchet invert *them?*" She had the DM-component in mind; and while the method used by the criminal had not been inversion, she wanted to lead Doré into the solid area.

136

"He would use the same principle as with the atomic flipping of the hollow ball: increase of intra-atomic repulsion at the outer surface, increase of attraction at the core, and so-on in between."

"So why is it a whole threshold-jump more difficult?"

"Two reasons. One is that in a solid there are more atoms and more thickness. But the other is a difficulty of principle. At the inside of the hollow ball, the number of surface atoms is only a fraction smaller than at the outside. But as between the surface and the core of a solid, the difference is almost infinite. That's a thing to get hold of, Claudine—and I haven't, and maybe I never will, maybe I'm not that bright."

Gazing at him, she said honestly: "I think you are. I think you can."

Frowning, he negated slowly. "I'm not sure I am or can."

"But—*he* could?"

"Greatest in the galaxy! Wonderful guy!" His eyes shone.

She was on the verge of slipping in another question about his identity. She decided against it: Jim had promised, and he would not tell, and she should not trick him into hinting. Besides, it was not directly pertinent: who Blanchet might be—that droll king?—was less important than the question of Doré's involvement.

Instead, she mused aloud: "So he could invert solids —probably both spherical and angular. And that's the very end in flipping."

"Not quite," he responded.

"Oh? There's something deeper?"

"There is. And he could do it."

"I just know you're going to tell me what it is."

"You lucky girl, of course I am. What's deepest of all —I think—is *electronic re-revving.*"

Her stomach-constrictions were painful. "It's a gay name, my friend. Tell me what it is."

"Changing the spin on an electron. In fact, changing the spins on the corresponding electrons in a whole lot of atoms all at once. That, Claudine, effects a qualitative

137

change in matter—not just a structural change. And Blanchet could do it—" He rattled on, not noticing her pallor, telling her how it was done and what it accomplished and how he had once seen Blanchet bring it off with a meter-diameter sphere of crystal that had been condensed to a fantastic degree of mass. . . .

She didn't know exactly when he finished talking about it. She was studying her wineglass. She became aware of his hand on hers. This dear man had come as close as he possibly could to telling her that he had all the know-how for inverting the hearts and re-revving the electrons in the DM; and with a kind of ultimate naiveté of veiled confession, he had disclaimed the ability to do what he knew how to do, projecting the ability on Blanchet—who, now she thought about it, could well be a fantasy.

With determination she gulped wine and confronted him, driving on to the next connection.

"I can see," she almost whispered, "why Blanchet would be a kind of second father to you."

"Second only in time, Claudine. First in priority."

She laid a hand on his hand on her hand. "You don't like your father, Jim?"

He closed his eyes hard. He shook his head once.

"You said he used to hypnotize you."

"The bugger can do it any time he wants."

She brooded over him, sorrowing. It wasn't a question of a conquerable weakness: this was a case where the father had established hypnotic mastery over the son and would keep it forever, unless . . .

"Then," she pressed, "you have been together?"

He looked up—his eyes were definitely wet. "I didn't get that."

"You and your father—you have been together on the ship?"

Wondering, he shook his head no.

She compressed her lips: this was terribly difficult. . . . "Listen, Jim," she tried. "A little while ago you said that telepsychic phenomena sneer at distance. Now, hypnosis is not in itself telepsychic; but thought can be tele-

138

psychically projected, and so perhaps can hypnosis. Tell me: would it be possible for your father to hypnotize you at a distance, when you didn't even know he was there?"

It reduced him to misery. He brooded while she pitied. Presently he said low: "He's done it."

With those three syllables he had forged the final link in the chain of possibles. Or, no: not precisely a chain with links intermeshed—rather, a neural circuit with synapses not quite in contact but almost unambiguously aiming at each other. Old Fire-Eyes had the motive: paranoid-apocalyptic doomsday: trigger the starborne Sodom and Gomorrah so that with stern poetic justice she would go radiant at the moment of peak velocity; build up the doomsday message in the terrified hearts of passengers and crew by mysteriously murdering first the captain, then the acting captain; and at climax, announce it all as Gawt's Doom and exhort them all to pray. Greco had demonstrated that he knew about the DM and the murders. It now appeared possible that Greco, at a distance, his presence not even known to his son, had hypnotized his son and steered him to do the Greco-will: first, perhaps before takeoff, changing the spin on the DM-electrons; second and third, inverting hearts. Jim had all but demonstrated his own competency to bring off this sophisticated flipping: he had denied that he *could* do the essential things—invert solids without snapping connected pipes, change electronic spin—but his master Blanchet, who *could* do those things, had taught him the theory of doing those things; and perhaps Greco *à distance* had been able to activate Doré hypnotically to put theory into practice. . . .

Squeezing both his hands, she urged: "Has he done it on this voyage?"

His hands squeezed back. "Maybe. I dunno. How would I know?"

"Have you—done anything goofy?"

His smile was tremulous. "Nothing too goofy for me to do all by myself—"

He lost the smile. "That is," he muttered, "nothing that I know about."

His head came up slowly, and he gazed at her with eyes flowing, but he held his mouth as firm as he could, and he said as steadily as he could: "It is not right for a man to be a slave to his father, Claudine."

The last guard melted, the last reticence dissolved. She stood beside him, a hand on his shoulder. Suddenly her arms went about his head and she mothered him against her, crooning to him, while both his arms clasped her waist and he clung to her for many seconds. . . .

His hands gripped her waist, and he thrust her away (but didn't let go) and stood up, looking down on her. "I don't often blow like that," he told her, "but I'd like to have you around every time I do. Why don't we get married?"

Her hands squeezed his arms just below the shoulders, her mouth was open, she stared into his great ingenuous eyes. She swallowed. She husked: "Excuse me, but I could have sworn I heard you say—"

"I did. Let's get married, Claudine. The captain can do it in the morning."

She began to shake him, mother-remonstrating. "You're crazy. You don't know me from beans—"

The tears were still there, his hands were tightening on her waist, his mouth was wonderful. "Yes I do," he insisted, "and I'm not crazy, I love you, I fell splat on my face when you tied my perfect score in the Gunnery-Aerie, it's the first time I've *loved* a girl since I was four years old. Please, Claudine? please?"

Her hands left his shoulders and slipped around his ribs, and she pressed her cheek against his chest much as she had done with the king, only this time it wasn't just *camaraderie;* she was laughing and crying, bedazed and bedazzled, and high on the arch of the rainbow that color-drenched her heart there was a bluebird singing. And now his great arms were around her shoulders, crowding her to him. Inside she wailed at herself: "Lieutenant St. Cyr, you damned fool, you're a cop, and *he did it,* he's a mass murderer, a maniac—"

His hand was brushing her hair. Timorously. Just a brushing touch.

From deep in her chest issued an *"Ohhh!"* She clung. She freed herself and stood back, half crouched before him, distraughtly brushing back hair-wisps.

She asserted in amazement: "My God—I *do* love you!"

Eagerly he demanded: "Then you *will?*"

Her head vaguely shook itself. "Are you maybe—transposing me, Jim? Or hypnosis, maybe?"

He had her in his arms again. "I swear I am not. It's the thing we read about and never know until it happens to both of us."

Prolonged silence. Both of them were trembling.

He uttered: "Claudine? Will you?"

Her mouth was against his chest, so her answer came out muffled, but it would have made no sense anyway.

His arms tightened. "With you I can be a free soul, Claudine. Isn't that ridiculous? getting married to be free?"

She was weeping, thinking miserably, weeping while she thought. Was he pulling a fast ploy—seeking to marry her so that as his wife she couldn't testify against him? No, no, she was convinced, no! Perhaps he suspected that he had been his father's tool, but she was intuitively satisfied that his candor was genuine: he didn't *know* this, he didn't *know* what he had done, he didn't know that he had done *any*thing. He wanted her to marry him because he wanted this, and it was all he meant.

His lips were on her hair. When his voice came, it was hushed and clear and true. "I want to kiss you. But not here. I want to walk with you on grass under stars, all alone in a great space, just as though we were sweethearts together in meadow starlight. And I want to kiss you there."

That one ruined her utterly. Near collapse, she clung to him, nodding her head a little.

He cried: "Let's go!"

"Go where?"

141

"The shooting gallery! Grass. Stars. Wide open spaces. All alone—"

She got out a handkerchief from wherever she kept it and dabbed at her eyes and nose. Standing away, she looked up at him, perplexed. "It's locked."

"Transposition laughs at locksmiths!"

"It's guarded."

"I'll hit 'em with a mesmer!"

He took her arm and got her started. She hurried along beside him, a lost soul en route to an impossible paradise.

18

There was absolutely no hurry. They strolled the darkened length of Frolic Street, deserted save for furtive amour-skulkers, like boy and girl heading through city streets for the park, coupled in the wonderful way that makes walking awkward and so enforces leisurely progress: her arm tight around his waist, his arm around her shoulders, her head nestled in his shoulder-hollow. He hardly knew when they left Frolic Street to enter narrow ship-corridors, and she did not know at all. They did not speak, except for an occasional minimum signal like "We go left here" or "Excuse, I have to sneeze."

If Claudine was now the least degree dubious of his love, she had preciously drowned the dubiety in her knowledge of the wonder of his love. Claudine loved him.

Nevertheless, as they approached the shooting gallery, again she was fuzzily, murkily conscious that she was compromising her duty, and she was groping toward means of justifying the compromise. Of course he was guilty—but wasn't he merely a zombie-tool of his dominating father? The man-murders and the ship-murder

142

could not be brushed off; but, committed under hypnotic influence and without responsible consciousness, they could be classified as acts of temporary insanity.

As for the DM-sphere, she would persuade Jim to deactivate it—if he still could. This would be a test of wife against father: this kind of test she had always despised, but in this case she was seeing the point in terms of Jim's permanent well-being. She would put it flatly to him as a test—but before marriage, not after: as a condition of marriage—and dear God, if he should fail the test, let her die with the *Eiland!* It would be for him his emancipation, his self-launching through love! Indeed, she now remembered with a flooding of joy, the murders could not be proved against him—even were he to confess, *he* could not prove them: perfect crimes they were! and as for the catabolium, she had only to bring him forward as the one who had the occupational capacity to deactivate it

if it were not too late

and although hard suspicion would therefrom fall upon him, nothing was provable. . . .

How long? Ten hours? *Could* she persuade him? My love, my love, you *must* be persuaded! Only—*could* she?

But of course she could! He hadn't *done* it on purpose—not even consciously! And once he realized that their love would be atomized if he didn't decontaminate the sphere, despite the mortal suspicion that it would cast upon him, he would gladly and swiftly

only

They approached the gallery door. His arm tightened about her. She was privately trying to frown out a puzzle that was hardening into semi-form in her mental fuzz. It amounted to this: whence would Greco have learned enough sophistication to communicate hypnotically to Jim the ideas of inverting hearts and re-revving electrons? And somehow implicated with this puzzle was another: if Blanchet were indeed aboard, who was he and what did it mean?

They stood interclasped before the door. Jim whispered: "Look, Ma—no hands." She thrilled with doubt-haunted devotion. He stared at the electronic lock: it flipped, the door vanished. He led her through, turned, and created the door again. Swinging, he conned the gloom: there were no guards evident.

He took her hand. They stood in springy grass in darkness that would have been total had it not been for the implacable brightness and multiplicity of stars in hard space. It was almost like full moonlight.

Their hands squeezed, their fingers interwove: nerve-to-nerve communion, intimate as the communion of two minds in one brain.

He said: "I love you, Claudine."

Again her eyes closed for a moment, and she knew herself, and herself was entirely his, and she breathed: "Jim, I *do* love you so—"

They watched stars.

He was strolling forward, drawing her languidly with him. "We are going to the exact center of this wide-open under-the-sky meadow. And there, all alone on grass and under raw stars, for the first time I am going to kiss you."

She washed the business out of her brain, clean. She let herself be drawn onward into the heart of this Elysium. She knew this love was real.

He stopped. "Center of the meadow," he said. He drew her around so that they faced each other, four hands clasped at arms' length, absorbing each other's nearly invisible eyes.

Unsteadily he said: "You are my life and all its meaning."

On her second try she got it out. "I will love you always."

He drew her to him. They embraced.

She was catapulted away from him, shocked by the shot. Stunned, she watched him waver down.

144

19

Grief comes later, always. First comes shock, with various instinctive or educated responses such as weeping and possibly clasping the corpse. Claudine was a cop, and almost instantly she knew he was dead, and she swung to the right toward the shot direction.

In dim distance, she thought she saw the muzzle of the Number Five Rifle in the Gunnery-Aerie rising to normal position. That was the rifle that yesterday morning had been fired by the king.

Police response, bereaved comprehension, and roaring anger all swirled into coda. The Claudine-puma, blood-hot, raced across the grass, entered the updraft, ascended into the Gunnery-Aerie, hit the floor ready to attack and gouge and knee and kill. Which she could do.

The killer had evidently left by the other exit as she had entered. No portholes to seek him through. No point in running to a gun to sweep the range below with its electronic sight—they were set so they couldn't be lowered that much, except by the crud who had just bloodied her Jim. Prowling the aerie, she found the other exit and whipped down the draft and panned 360 degrees.

Whoever it was, was gone.

Still panther-bounding, Claudine whipped up the updraft again; and now she patterned on what she had subliminally sensed—a somehow-familiar smoke-aroma. Cigar smoke. The aerie was dark. She went to where she thought the controls must be, and she tried switches until the red illumination came on; and then she went back to the gunposts and swept the aerie, looking for anything.

A tiny object on the floor caught her eye. She ran to it, stooped, picked it up, scrutinized it.

A cigar band . . .

The aroma was diabolically known.

Back she went to the control board, and tried switches again, and presently found one that yielded white light. Under this light she looked at the cigar band.

It said: SODIM E GOMORRH. Gold lettering on a white ground.

Dozens of puzzle-pieces fell sickeningly into place, in the midst of this tragic moment when the last thing her broken heart wanted was to solve puzzles.

Closing her eyes, she pressed her back against a wall and fought down her gorge and comprehended that her legs were going limp and she was slumping. Her head went hard down, and she frowned her blood back into action. Opening her eyes, she pushed herself away from the wall and forced herself to do some rhythmic deep breathing. Then she self-tested: she was in control.

Looking swiftly around, she found the intercom and went to it. Since this was a crew station, presumably it was a restricted crew-com. Opening it, she said quietly into it: "Lieutenant St. Cyr calling Captain Mashti and Lieutenant Brh and Chief Tuli. Over."

After a surprising five repetitions at five-second intervals came a hard female reply: "Tuli here."

Claudine said dead: "Report immediately to the shooting gallery. Emergency. Send men to bring Captain Mashti and Lieutenant Brh. Also, send men to bring Commander Hastings and medics and a litter. Over."

The voices of Mashti and Brh came in blending variously, the general sense of both messages being: "I heard it, I am coming. Out."

Tuli said: "Coming. Out."

Disconnecting, Claudine leaned against the wall again. *Out. Out.*

Puma no longer, just plain gutted woman, she stumbled to the downdraft, returned to the grass, and picked her way to the place where she had left her lover.

146

Kneeling beside him, she got out a pocket lamp and flashed it on his head and cut out the light very fast.

Then deliberately she lay down in the grass beside him, her face by his ruined head, and took one of his hands in both of hers, and talked to him:

"I love you, Jim. You loved me, Jim. You had nothing to do with any of this. Your father had nothing to do with any of this. It would have been *good*, Jim—"

He shuddered.

She was on her knees, bending over him, her head against his chest. His heartbeat was feeble, but there it was. Cautiously, using her handkerchief, she examined his bloody head.

The bullet had not broken it open. The bullet had only creased it.

Leaping to her feet, she stared toward the door of the Gunnery-Aerie. *Come,* medics! *Come* . . .

Her lips went tight together. Dead or alive, Jim had been shot with intent to kill.

She knew where she had smelled the exquisite cigar-bouquet. She knew who knew she would be with Jim.

20

Mashti stood by, in the fine pomp of command ineffectuality, while Brh and Claudine and Tuli and three male yeomen of Claudine's crew moved with grim efficiency about the police work. In place of Dr. Hastings, a doctor-lieutenant appeared with medics: he supervised first aid (mainly, a shot of adrenaline), and the critical patient was removed with gentle haste. Claudine stood quietly watching the litter go away: she wanted to follow, but there was a little matter of police business. She must trust the doctor.

After her sleeve had been gently plucked for the third time, she noticed the plucking. It was Tuli, who said nothing. Claudine shrugged and went back to supervision of the duty.

In a little while Tuli and a yeoman returned from the aerie, and Tuli reported to Claudine: "That seems to be what we can do, miss."

"Very good, Chief," Claudine intoned. "Get with it in the laboratory."

"How about the king, miss?"

' "I'll be with him."

"Miss, excuse me—I saw how it was. If you'd rather—"

Claudine wearily negated. "I have a thing to see him about."

Tuli nodded and stepped back.

Brh stood questioning before Claudine. Not meeting his eyes, she suggested: "Why don't you inform Greco about his son's accident, but keep holding him in the brig. As far as I'm concerned, he's clear, but he's a nuisance when he's free."

They *all* had seen how it was. Brh inquired reticently: "Are you ready to tell me why he's clear?"

Mashti quietly joined them.

Mouth and brows tight, Claudine shook her head in a positive no.

Over her head, Brh and Mashti exchanged glances. "Later, then," agreed the lieutenant. "Captain, shall we go now?"

Mashti too was tight-lipped. He spoke hard to Claudine: "Lieutenant, I expect a full report in thirty minutes. In my cabin."

Brh froze.

Claudine said low: "Captain, as you once remarked, I am under your command only in a restricted way. Just now I am in command of an investigation for the Galactic Police."

Mashti's lips loosened and began to work. Then he

148

burst out: "But how about that God-damned DM? Suren says it's irreversible! It's only *hours* now—"

Brh risked his career by saying: "Captain, in my opinion, we now celebrate or radiate on Lieutenant St. Cyr. I respectfully suggest that we leave her alone now."

Staring at him, Mashti blurted: *"Mis-ter Brh!"*

"Don't call her," Brh added. "Let her call us."

Mashti achieved a violent internal decision. "Lieutenant Brh," he commanded, "follow me." He broke for the distant door.

Brh hesitated.

Claudine's dreary voice barely reached his ears. "Lieutenant—"

He swung to her. "Miss St. Cyr?"

"I asked for Dr. Hastings. Why did his lieutenant come instead?"

Rigidly Brh responded: "Dr. Hastings is dead, miss."

"Well! And how did he die?"

"Suicide, miss. We don't know why."

Claudine's head hung: she was not quite trembling. "Tell me what time."

"Early this evening. His lieutenant has not yet done a post mortem, but he estimates the time between 1800 and 2200 hours."

"Very good, Lieutenant." Pause. "Excuse the expression, I am not quite myself."

"I understand. Call me when you need me."

Mashti hovered distantly and threateningly by the door.

"Go mend your fences," Claudine told Brh with a wan smile. "I think you are a good man."

At her head-jerk, Tuli came up. Tuli seemed somewhat hangdog.

"How about the king?" demanded Claudine.

Tuli definitely wilted. She replied crisply, yet with strain: "I have to advise you that I cannot answer for the king after about 2300 hours."

"That's about four hours ago. Why not?"

"Miss, I fell asleep."

"How did you happen to do that?"

"He made me."

Claudine inhaled, and exhaled, and decided that she was being grinned upon by a skull. She pressed: "Is he in his suite now?"

Tuli, her blood pressure evidently about eighty over fifty, stated: "Miss, I do not know."

"Why not? Didn't you check the light signals?"

"Miss, in my haste to—collect myself and come, I—forgot."

Claudine's voice was very soft. "Your first time with a man, Tuli?"

"Practically."

"Before he left you, I hope he had the grace to cover you."

"With an afghan, yes."

"Good man. Four men were supposed to be on guard in the corridor, Tuli. Did any of them see him depart?"

Tuli's brows were down hard. "Which do you want first, miss—my reply, or my stripes?"

Claudine's voice went strange. "He is a most unusual man, Tuli. Please forget this incident, because I have forgotten it. Please go now to supervise the laboratory work."

"Yes, miss. Do you wish to tell me where I can find you if something emerges?"

"With the king, Tuli. With the king. If he is there, that is."

Then slowly, head down, she strolled toward the door. Strolled firmly, though. No wavering. She knew where she was going. She knew now, assuming certain eliminations, who the criminal was.

Her ultimate purpose was a counter-kill.

Part Four

SODIM E GOMORRH

21

She stumped through corridors until her subconscious had led her to her room; and she let herself in, and locked herself in, and stood in the geometric center of her floor for thirteen seconds.

Her head came decisively up for the first time in many minutes. The middle signal light near the ceiling indicated that the king was in his bedroom. She went to the phone and spoke the king's number. Ten pale-pink light flashes told her that the phone had chimed low without a response. Then ten strong amber flashes said that the chime had gone loud. Then a fast-oscillating bright flash asserted that a gong had started to grind—and, boy, she heard it through the door!

It cut off fast, though. A sleepy-angry male servant voice demanded: "What is it?"

"St. Cyr here. Tell the king I will call on him in ten minutes."

"But—at only 0330 hours?"

"Nine minutes and fifty-six seconds. Get him up. Out." She disconnected.

Barely time to change bloodied clothing and go into the corridor and question the guards.

No guard had seen the king leave or reenter since long before midnight. Meaningless, actually: *this* villain must be able to deploy hypnosis more deftly than Greco!

Grimly, ironically, she watched her antique Jaeger-LeCoultre while it ticked away seconds—backward. She reentered her room and locked the corridor door. On the instant, she opened *his* door and entered his salon.

A little way in, the king stood facing her. He wore a royal blue dressing gown. The color struck her as being ironic. Capping the irony viciously, she marched past him and sat at the little table where yesterday they had enjoyed luncheon. After a moment's hesitation, he came and sat opposite her.

She watched the table: her thoughts were already collected, it was composure that she was collecting.

He produced a cigar. "May I?"

She had to glance up to see what he meant. When she saw, she shuddered with profound revulsion and looked down again, nodding. One of his foliaceous white eyebrows went up, but presently he lit the cigar. When the smoke drifted around her, again she shuddered and then went still.

He said gravely: "I could comment that you seem distraught. Instead, I will merely ask you to begin."

She looked up and hard-faced him. "I'll begin," she said formally, "by reviewing events of pertinent interest during this voyage."

"I am attentive."

"On our first afternoon, while I was being promenaded by the king who regarded himself as the most beloved ruler in the galaxy, a man from his own planet tried to assassinate him. On the very next day, the news came through that this king had been deposed by a powerful coalition junta of white and golden Ligerians, and that he would be hunted down and assassinated. This king accepted both events with total sangfroid. I suggest that the news of his deposition came as no surprise—that he had expected this prior to the embarkation and perhaps even prior to purchasing the *Eiland of Ligeria.*"

She waited. He had whitened a little, but he merely replied: "Pray continue."

"On our first evening also, I was taken by this king to watch a performance by the Great Doré, a young man in whom the king singularly expressed the most profound interest—a young man uncommonly talented at psycho-

154

kinetic transposition and inversion. Doré later told me that his mentor, a man stage-named Blanchet, was the most talented inverter in the galaxy—could invert and revert even solids, had been known to invert the head of a golf stick without snapping off the stick, and could even re-rev electrons in atoms."

"Did Doré reveal the real name of this Blanchet?"

"You know that he did not."

"How do I know?"

"Well—he did not. But more events, Your Majesty. That same afternoon, we discovered that the DM-component had been tampered with; and Commander Suren later deduced that its core-composition had been altered from normal elastium to potentially radiant catabolium by re-revving the inner-orbit electrons just before or just after take off, a thing that could be accomplished only by the most advanced psychokinetic technique imaginable. Doré has adequately coached me on this theory. The effect was, of course, to convert the DM into a self-irradiating device which would convert the ship into a star just as the ship reached peak velocity—and which now will go anyway in a few hours, even though we are in freefall.

"Captain Schwarz, who somehow understood a way to neutralize this effect, was murdered at dinner that night: his heart was psychokinetically inverted. Subsequently Commander Swainson let it be known that he, too, knew how to do it: he was murdered next morning: *his* heart was psychokinetically inverted.

"You are now free to comment, if you wish."

The king critically examined the length of the blue-gray ash on his cigar tip. "I prefer that you be the one to come to the point."

"Then let me remind you of one more event series, part of which will be news to you. On our first afternoon, when I crawled under the DM-component, I found a label adhering to the lattice beneath the sphere. This label said SODIM E GOMORRH."

Cigar in mouth, the king gazed at her and waited.

"This red herring turned my thoughts to Greco; and

the next day, by one of those cosmic coincidences that louse up history, Greco gave us loud reason to believe that he knew about the murders and the ship sabotage. I had theorized, from Greco's paranoid structure, that if he were guilty, he would have deliberately planted the label as a sort of cryptic signature-warning, and that ultimately he would have to reveal himself as a necessary consummation; and apparently he did so. That night, when I went to see Doré—well, why review this? you *know* what Doré told me."

"If I do, admit that you have kept reviewing other things that I already knew."

"All right. I'll play it out, then. I thought I might establish that Doré, the illegitimate son of Greco, had been Greco's tool; and in fact, what he told me established that this could have been a possibility under hypnosis. However, the—some other—rather abrupt considerations have caused me to clear Greco entirely. There are too many inconsistent elements in the psychological pattern —for instance, the plain fact that Greco is too ignorant and stupid to conceive any of the three crimes in question."

"I agree wholeheartedly. This is a sensible elimination. Then?"

"The criminal, Your Majesty, is Blanchet."

"Who?"

"Blanchet. Doré's master flipper."

"He is aboard?"

"Doré did not deny it."

"And why Blanchet?"

"All the things that Doré told me about Blanchet have fallen into pattern; I have all of a sudden comprehended the man's character, and it is a rare sort of personality indeed—not rare in kind, but rare in power. If there were more than one aboard a ship having a complement of two thousand, it would be a miracle. And it is precisely the personality that would commit precisely these crimes in precisely this way, given the motivating situation—a situation that would motivate precisely this mind to bring off the major ship-irradiation and the incidental murders.

156

"Blanchet is indeed paranoid, a little, but it is not the guilt-ridden apocalyptic paranoia of Greco. Rather, Blanchet is a potent psychopath—an expansive, colorful, powerful, richly attractive, complex, restless, regally dramatic paranoid-schizoid psychopath. He has overdramatized and identified himself with the current crisis-situation, and so he has gone intelligently berserk—with total sangfroid, mind you: it is characteristic of the breed. His inward dramatics led him to sign his prime crime with the SODIM E GOMORRH label, and they will lead him to reveal himself and his actions to all of us—as soon as he is convinced that the catabolium reaction is finally irreversible so that nobody can somehow force him to abort it. He *must* announce, so that there will be an hour or so of hysterical appreciation by his two thousand victims of doom—not for cruelty, but because the act must be savored to be meaningful."

Pause.

The king told her soberly: "Again I applaud, Claudine—I think your analysis of this personality is right without exception, and doubtless the criminal is Blanchet. May I ask one or two questions?"

"If it will expedite this business," she spat back.

"What business is to be expedited?"

"Blanchet must reveal himself immediately, so that he can be persuaded to abort the catabolium before it is too late."

"How do you know it is not already too late?"

"Blanchet has not revealed himself."

"Eh . . . Well: how could the Sodim e Gomorroh label be interpreted as a signature? What is the connection with Blanchet?"

"You tell me."

"I cannot imagine what to tell you. You tell me."

"Later, if you force me to it."

"All right. Next question. You said that Blanchet is motivated by a current crisis-situation. And I think you are now required to specify what the situation is—and how it affects Blanchet—and therefore, who Blanchet is."

He had laid down his cigar; they were eye to eye, her color was minimal, his pallor was ultimate.

She said deliberately: "If Blanchet were a king whose planet was about to depose him, he might conclude to die sublimely in space; and because the ship that he would be destroying in the process could be considered an empress —the *Eiland of Ligeria*—it would be aesthetically right for two thousand consorts to die with her in the grandest *bradzh* in Ligerian history."

Silence.

Fingering his dying cigar in the ashtray, the king said softly: "I think you are obligated to extend the identification of Blanchet with Zhavàr somewhat more circumstantially."

"Gladly. Well, not gladly, but willingly. I should point out, though, that the catabolium is speeding its breeding. Feel free to stop me whenever you are satisfied."

"Thank you."

"Blanchet offered his show exclusively to an aristocratic audience in the royal palace of Ligeria, and only one weekend each year: it is a thing that a king would do. He called the show-team Blanchet and Doré, that is to say, White and Gold, the planetary colors—again, a king-thing. It was Blanchet who got the unknown Doré top billing on the *Eiland of Ligeria:* this makes Blanchet a top-hole notable—for instance, a king. Ready to interrupt, Your Majesty?"

"Candidly, I am going to wait until you get it all out. This is fascinating."

"Superior paranoid-schizoid: classic case! Now I will tie-in events. The man who sabotaged the DM had to be able to re-rev electrons: Blanchet. The man who murdered Schwarz and Swainson had to be able to invert hearts—a complex meld of hollow and solid inversion involving high-level anatomical knowledge—without snapping off the pipes: again, Blanchet. The DM had to be sabotaged either just before or just after takeoff: the night before is a possibility—and I did not report to you until 0700 hours on embarkation day—and Blanchet unquestionably could hypnotically neutralize a skeleton guard on

158

the engine room. To murder Schwarz, Blanchet had to be *there:* you were sitting next to him. To murder Swainson, Blanchet had to be *there:* you were beside me in the Gunnery-Aerie; you unaccountably missed a shot just about the moment when Swainson died—and you an expert—possibly because you had swiftly inverted the electronic sight in order to evil-eye Swainson below in the midst of the shooting. Your Majesty, are you familiar with the logic of multiplicative probabilities?"

Long, long silence.

The king drew a small proton-gun and leveled it at her skull. "I'll bet all these insights would die with you—wouldn't they, Claudine?"

"Oui."

"Why should I not kill these insights?"

"You will not—because they validate your signature."

"If I announce—as you say I will do—that will be validation enough. But killing you now will delay the revelation—a thing that I wish, as you say."

"But why be so messy, Zhavàr? Why not just invert my heart?"

"Eh," he agreed, nodding thoughtfully, pocketing the gun. "And thank you for finally calling me Zhavàr. But on the other hand—why, by inverting your heart, should I establish myself as the criminal? For as yet you have not demonstrated that I can flip."

"This I am about to do. On Frolic Street, you inadvertently flipped my wristwatch."

He started. "I did?"

She uncovered it and showed him. "It was positively running normally after the gold watchmaker wound it. Outside, you inspected it. Next time I looked, it was running backward. In between, nobody looked at it."

Preening his moustache with a forefinger, he inspected the ceiling. "Dashed careless monarch."

"You won't give in *yet?*"

"Perhaps I am playing with you, to gain time on my *bradzh.*"

She went vicious. "Blanchet smokes Sodim e Gomorrh cigars. *You* smoke Sodim e Gomorrh cigars."

"So now we have the signature linkage. But what makes you think that I smoke them? I told you that mine are made for me specially, they are unbanded—see?" He produced a nude cigar and showed her.

She surveyed its length with scorn. "Any ass can shuck off the bands and call them special. Sorry, Your Majesty: I know the bouquet."

"Good woman. *Mea culpa,* it is my royal peccadillo. But they are *almost* made special for me: I buy them from the watchmaker, and he has them made special for *him*. Planetary colors, you know. *Sodim e Gomorrh—* White and Gold. You saw his wild cigar counter."

She was frowning: something way down was bugging her postern antennae.

"But how," he added, "do you know that Blanchet smokes them?"

Anger-adrenaline flooded her. She erupted vitriol: "Because, you stinking bastard, you were smoking one in the Gunnery-Aerie when you shot my lover!"

Slowly his head came up, brows hard down, eyes beginning to smolder. "When I did *what?*"

"Merciful God," she grated, "hold me back from strangling him, keep me patient while I try to convince him that it is no good dodging it. Listen, Zhavàr. Only you and Tuli knew that I liked Doré, that I would be in his room. You were Doré's old master, Blanchet—you were my spurned would-be lover, Zhavàr—it was double blasphemy against your love-charisma. And so you phoned his room while I was there; and when he answered, *you* knew how to bug the phone—with your cigar-lighter, or with PK, who cares? You froze the switch so the line would stay open when he disconnected. And so, listening, you learned about our"— her voice broke, and she angrily controlled it—"our love and our plans. So you poled-over the corridor guards with hypnotism—you'd already poled-over Tuli—and hurried to the shooting gallery and—waited, and—shot him."

She clamped her jaw shut and sat trying to freeze its trembling, but her deadly eyes never left his eyes.

Slowly he rose to his feet. Leaning heavily over her, he ejaculated: *"Doré* has been *shot?"*

The spirit went out of her. Eyes down, she droned: "Your affectation of innocence would deceive anybody else."

"You *loved* him?"

"Didn't you believe your own eavesdropping?"

Dropping back into his chair, he gripped the table. "I did not do that. I *would* not do that."

"I don't believe you."

"Why not?"

"The man who shot Doré is the same man who murdered two captains and sabotaged the ship. I know this. The man is Blanchet. Blanchet is you. You had the reason to kill Doré—a double reason: to delay discovery, to prevent love. You had the ability to learn that we would be there, the ability to enter the locked gallery, the ability to invert the gun to fire downward, the ability to shoot straight in semidarkness. And you were smoking your cigar."

"And you are about to avenge him."

"I wish to persuade you to neutralize the DM. To do this, I am trying to keep from killing you with my hands. Which I could do."

"Have you checked fingerprints on the rifle?"

"Tuli collected them. She is now analyzing them. There will, however, be only one set: yours: some from yesterday, some from just now. The guns were wiped clean before we used them yesterday, and they have not subsequently been used—except by you, just now."

"You could give me the benefit of the doubt, until you know."

"And if it does prove that there is only one set of prints?"

He spread hands. "The other fellow used gloves." Again he gripped the table, leaning forward, his face rarely passionate. "Claudine—I did *not* shoot him. I *would* not."

Their eyes for a silent while were steadily engaged.

161

Somberly she asserted: "I want to believe you about Doré. But—all the other things?"

He drew another cigar—and started to put it away again. "Smoke it," she said quietly, "I don't fetish." "Thank you," he told her lighting it. He puffed thoughtfully.

Then, cocking his head up, he remarked: "I couldn't transpose a couple of grapes."

22

In seven words—if they were true—he had obliterated every smidgin of her case against him.

It was her turn to be standing, looking down on him. She demanded: "If I can't prove that you *have* this ability, how can you prove that you *lack* it?"

"With a probe. I volunteer to submit."

"And if you invert the probe?"

His brows arched. "That I didn't think of. I couldn't prove that I hadn't, could I?"

She eased into the chair, earnestly studying his eyes. "But you are telling the truth?"

"I am."

"I have already said that you are paranoid-schizoid. You people lie with great ease and conviction."

"I suggest that your less fruitless course would be to believe me. I shall continue to deny the crimes and the flipping ability until the ship goes radiant. If you believe me, you will start looking elsewhere—and you may find something, though I doubt it."

"Why do you doubt it?"

"Because you are convinced that Blanchet is the guilty one, and because you have the character of Blanchet pegged so neatly. I am not mocking, Claudine: I have known him for many years, quite intimately, and your analysis of his personality is frighteningly accurate. Now think, Claudine: *who else* aboard this ship could be Blanchet? What was it you said about him? No, wait, I'll quote you: I don't think well, but I remember well. 'Blanchet is a potent psychopath—an expansive, colorful, powerful, richly attractive, complex, restless, regally dramatic paranoid-schizoid—' "

Claudine suddenly leaned across the table and clutched his wrist with both hands, adding: "—A notable habitué of society pages and gossip columns—affairs of the heart and of the blood—annual disappearances—rumors that he was secretly a prince or a narcotics king or a star ballet dancer on one or another planet—actually a flipper for the King of Ligeria, *hein?* called himself Blanchet because it was the opposite of Schwarz, *hein?* of *course* the ship's captain had enough drag with the ship's captain to get Doré star booking—"

He waited, watching her face change.

She said positively: "I was right: Blanchet re-revved the DM. Blanchet was Schwarz, and Schwarz was the imaginative paranoid-schizoid driven intelligently berserk by ultimate crisis: his beloved mistress the *Eiland of Ligeria,* was being raped off the spaceways to be reprocessed as industrial scrap. So she had to die by his hand during a space run—her last—and he with her. But the two thousand people, Zhavàr—the *bradzh*—certainly he had the spectacular imagination and the cold blood to do it, but could there be a positive motive? How could he have soaked up enough primitive culture-obsession to motivate a *bradzh* during two or three weeks a year in your super-civilized palace?"

"He was the son of my older sister."

"He was Ligerian? Not German? Is *that* why I can't get anything on his first twenty years?"

"His mother was widowed when he was a small child," the king recalled. "I foster-fathered him. He was brilliant, he was always a small edition of his adult self. He was also moody. When he was twelve, I made the mistake of taking him on a planetary tour. He fell in love with the old ways of the golden ones. Two years later he ran away. When he returned at eighteen, he was already the greatest master of transposition that I had ever seen; but he brought back with him a rocking ambivalence between hyper-urbanity and primitive culture-obsession. We stayed friends, but I soon got it that there was ambivalence in his affection for me: he loved me as a father, he hated me because he thought that my existence as king prevented his mother from being the planetary matriarch-empress. Soon I—used pressure to get him a commission in the Galactic Navy: it got him away from Ligeria, except for his annual visits. You know or surmise the rest, I imagine. He changed his name and Germanized himself for total anonymity—it was the other way of what you guessed: he chose Schwarz because it was the opposite of his childhood nickname, Blanchet, Whitey. I promised him that I would respect this anonymity; and until now, I have done so. Even after his death, I have done so. What good would it have done, Claudine, for me to tell you that the only man aboard who could possibly have re-revved the DM was Captain Schwarz—when Captain Schwarz was entirely too dead to help matters?"

One of her hands had stayed gently on his wrist. "So we are both bereaved, Zhavàr—unless Jim should chance to survive this. Why do you tell me about it now? It still can't save the ship."

He said bitterly: "Perhaps I am blackening the name of my nephew who is dead in order to clear myself who am alive."

She pressed his hand and was silent, frowning down.

He said: "We are losing time—and you are starting to make me want to gain it again. Bypass my bereavement, as you have bypassed your own crisis. Please think, Claudine."

She glanced up, gave him a swift weak smile, and looked down again. "We start then, Zhavàr, with the hypothesis that it was Blanchet-Schwarz who bombed the ship. But Schwarz assuredly did not invert his own heart; and since he was dead, he could not have inverted Swain-

164

son's heart, nor could he have inverted the rifle to shoot Jim. Zhavàr, we *cannot* assume that there is still *another* man on this ship who has Blanchet's capabilities—can we? Not Doré—he was cleared by the attack upon him. Not Greco—he's too stupid. Are we then back with Mashti and Suren again? But no; for neither of them would have had any reason to commit the murders unless he had sabotaged the DM, and it was surely Schwarz who did *that*—"

She looked up at him with swift suspicion: "Unless—" Again she smiled wanly: "I know, that's a fruitless trail." Frowning: "But what is fruitful?"

"I do not know."

"Zhavàr, it *cannot* have been Schwarz who ruined the DM; for I am morally certain that the same man committed all four crimes—there is positively no intuitive doubt of that in my mind. And since Schwarz was dead before he could do the last three, someone else who is still alive must have done all four."

"I assure you that if there is anyone else in the galaxy with the capacity to re-rev electrons and invert hearts, the improbability of his presence on this ship is astronomical."

"Then—"

"If you wish, I will be glad to phone Tuli and Brh, and we can—"

"Wait!" she begged, closing her eyes and pressing knuckles against temples.

Sodim e Gomorrh . . .

White and gold. Ligerian colors. Striped cigar counter. Good cigars and old watches. Schwarz flirted with me: could *that* mean that he . . .

Eyes closed, knuckling temples, she stayed at it while he watched with fascination. In her mind the memory-eidols were blubbing-up like Yellowstone mud-geyserlings: no associations yet, no formed reason for association— but intuitively she knew that they were all related: she had gone all inward-loose, to lure them. . . .

The captain or any sharp member of the crew would know how to bug a phone. . . .

But *dead:* inverted heart!

Her eyes came half open, the fingers of both hands rested on the table edge: she slowly, lightly beat the table edge with the fingers of one hand, her head swung from side to side a little, her eyes were glazed. He shared her semi-trance.

But *dead* . . .

Something.

Nothing?

Her eyes closed again, her hands stayed on the table.

Ligerian assassin escaped early yesterday morning, nowhere to be found.

Bodies of Schwarz and Swainson inspected at about 1100 hours.

Subsequently, Dr. Hastings a suicide . . .

Her eyes flew wide open. She spat at the king: "With Schwarz, Hastings played poker!"

In a motion he was on his feet. "I think you have it. What is it?"

"I want to verify a thing before I tell you. Will you come with me to the morgue?"

"Of course, only—"

"I know, you should dress first. Go ahead. How long?"

"Two minutes forty-seven seconds."

"Make it four. I have to talk with Tuli."

"You won't give me a preview of what you want to verify?"

"Only this much. I think we probably have three murders on our hands, all right—but not necessarily the three we thought."

23

Claudine prowled swiftly astern, tailed by the king, Mashti, Brh, Tuli, and two of her plainclothes yeomen. She led the way to the infirmary without regard for protocol, concentrating. There she was met by the same medical lieutenant who had officiated at the preliminary examination and removal of Doré. Since he knew her, she merely demanded: "First of all, how is Mr. Doré?"

"Critical," the doctor responded. "We are doing everything. But it is mainly concussion and shock and some hairline fractures. He has a good chance."

Having tossed up a fast mental *"Merci!"* she snapped: "Good. Now, Lieutenant—I want to see the bodies of Captain Schwarz and Commander Swainson."

Startled, the lieutenant looked at Mashti, who nodded. The lieutenant then asserted: "They may not be very presentable."

"Explain."

"Dr. Hastings personally removed both of them, with the aid of our light tractor beams, directly from autopsy to the morgue. I have not inspected them."

"I will inspect them." Vaguely half-conscious of the others, she added: *"We* will inspect them. Pray take us there."

"I have only three thermal suits. The morgue is deep-freeze."

She turned, addressing Mashti. "The lieutenant must wear one, and I must wear another. Captain, properly you should come; but it is imperative that the king be the third—and that is how it will be. If you wish to remain

167

behind and inspect independently afterward, that is your option."

Mashti got his mouth indignantly open. Brh laid a hand on his arm. Mashti got his mouth indignantly shut.

"Take us," Claudine said to the lieutenant. He shrugged and led the way to an anteroom, where he handed thermal suits to Claudine and the king and began to don one himself.

Dressing, she inquired: "Did you assist at either autopsy, Doctor?"

"Only with Commander Swainson."

"Why not with Captain Schwarz?"

"Dr. Hastings told us that Captain Schwarz was a special friend, and we knew this. He wished to perform the autopsy himself alone, as a—well, you know. So we stayed away."

"What about Commander Swainson?"

"In his case, Dr. Hastings did ask for my assistance—mine only, he specified."

"I will ask you later about his procedure, just as a formality. Are we ready, Doctor?" Intercom equipment prevented her voice from being muffled by the face-plate of the thermal suit.

"Ready, miss. Your Majesty?"

"Lead on, Doctor."

The lieutenant led them into the morgue, closing the thermal doors behind. They were aware of no temperature change. The morgue was simply a metal-walled room about four meters square, with sixteen drawers in one wall—enough, one would expect, even for a peak load.

Claudine ordered: "Commander Swainson first."

The lieutenant pressed a button, and the second drawer from the bottom in row three rolled out. Swainson lay there, sheet-covered, quick-frozen, only his eyes-closed head and neck exposed.

After a mere glance, Claudine asserted: "I would identify him positively as Swainson. Your Majesty?"

"Yes, from a short acquaintance."

"Doctor?"

"Yes, miss. No question."

168

"Close the drawer, and show us Captain Schwarz."

Swainson rolled away, and Schwarz rolled forth—second from the bottom in row two: sheet-covered, quick-frozen, only his eyes-closed head and neck exposed.

Him Claudine examined more carefully. Presently she inquired: "Your Majesty?"

"Captain Schwarz, beyond question."

"You are the one who best would know."

"I think so."

"Doctor?"

"No question, miss."

"May I borrow your cigar lighter, Your Majesty?"

Only for two seconds did the king stare at her. Then he observed: "After a moment's reflection, perhaps you will see the difficulty."

"Well, yes: the thermal suit. For the moment, then—Doctor, be good enough to pull back the sheet. All the way."

"But, miss—"

"Police officer, Doctor. I rarely faint at the sight of a man."

Grinning behind his face-plate, the lieutenant pulled back the sheet—and his shocked gasp rasped in his intercom.

After a brief inspection, the king mumbled: "Excuse me while I get out my lighter." He left the room, closed the door, and unzipped in normal temperature while, within the morgue-room deep-freeze, the doctor in consternation and the detective with composure contemplated the slight, short, nude golden body of the man who wore the face and blonde hair and blue eyes of Captain Schwarz.

Back came the king, handing her the lighter. She triggered it, weaving it above the face of the corpse. The face shriveled and vanished, giving place to another—the deep-frozen face of the golden Ligerian assassin.

But his eyes stayed blue, because of their contact lenses.

Emerging from the morgue, they found Mashti and
169

Brh and Tuli and the two yeomen in the anteroom. Claudine spoke crisply as she undressed:

"Captain Schwarz was not murdered—instead, he faked death by an old Ligerian *guru* trick: self-suspended animation. Once he was safely alone with Hastings in the autopsy room, Hastings let him out by a back door that the lieutenant here knows about. Schwarz forced the compliance of Hastings by threatening to tell the crew that Hastings was welshing on poker debts which presumably were enormous—a threat that compulsive Hastings could not sustain. The same night, or early the next morning, Hastings realized that he would soon be asked to show the body, and he got in touch with Schwarz. The captain wanted to choose his own time for self-revelation, he had to delay discovery until it would be clearly too late to reverse the DM-reaction. He therefore entered the brig anteroom—this is merely sound supposition—and hypnotized the guard and used PK to open the cell door and free the golden Ligerian; he then brought the Ligerian to the infirmary and blackmailed Hastings into deep-freezing the guy. Schwarz then created a strontilite Schwarz-mask for the poor little pigeon, and Hastings put him into autopsy—where the king and I innocently viewed him yesterday morning. Subsequently Dr. Hastings was overwhelmed with remorse and killed himself."

Brh muttered: "He *could* have waited to be irradiated with the rest of us."

"That isn't the point," the king clipped out. "The point is, that Schwarz is alive, and is our criminal—and Schwarz has perhaps the capability of saving the ship."

"Right," said Claudine absently: she was thinking.

Mashti demanded: "Can you prove that?"

"Stow that!" Brh roared. "The big thing now is—*where is Schwarz?*"

Deliberately Claudine consulted her backward-running Jaeger-LeCoultre. "I think I know," she told them.

As she led them out into the corridor and off in the direction of Frolic Street, Yeoman Gringle fell in beside Tuli. "Chief," he muttered, "I have the dope on that piece of paper."

170

"What piece of paper?"

"The one you handed me last night. The little white and gold paper. It's a cigar band. In English, it means White and Gold."

Head down, Tuli marched along a few steps. Then she merely said: "Very good, Gringle. Stay with us."

24

Deserted Frolic Street at 0530 hours was weird under hard stars, like a wartime Pigalle before dawn but hours after the last métro. Like a small combat patrol the eight eased along the left *chaussée* in the shop shadows: Claudine, the king, Mashti, Brh, Tuli, and three yeomen in close-order single file, until they approached the counterguarded clock shop. Claudine paused by the central counter, and the others gathered: ironically, it was the white-and-gold-striped cigar counter whose one and only brand was Sodim e Gomorrh—made of choice Ligerian tobaccos, sold under several brand names to select dealers on several planets, sold under the special Sodim e Gomorrh label to the watchmaker aboard the *Eiland of Ligeria*—who in turn distributed them to the *Eiland*'s several tobacco concessions and privately to the king's valet—who unbanded them before delivering them to the king.

Having gathered her party, Claudine motioned for silence and went to the shop door and quietly tried the old-fashioned doorknob. "Locked," she whispered.

Stepping forward, Brh said: "I have a master key to Frolic Street."

"Please give it to me," she requested, "and also your ship's master electronic key, since the inner door locks may be modern. Then all of you wait here—don't follow unless I call."

"Why?" asked Mashti.

"Because he can kill with a glance. We don't want to use force, we want to use persuasion. We have a ship to save, and he has to do it."

The king took her arm. "Then let me go in. You know why."

"I know that he desires me and is ambivalent toward you. I have a two-thirds chance, you have only half a chance. The difference in odds is significant. Stay out, Your Majesty, and the rest of you—that's a Galactic Police order."

In she went, and the door closed behind her—but they noticed that she had left it unlocked.

Gumshoeing through the dark abandoned clock shop, acquiring night eyes as she went, Claudine sneaked behind the rear counter and paused before the low door to the watchmaker's inner sanctum. She meditated. Once in her youth she had come up quietly on a paranoid friend and said "Boo!" and he had murderously grabbed her throat. Therefore she now called out to the closed door: "Lieutenant St. Cyr here. Let me in."

No answer.

She pushed: the door was locked. She tried the electronic key: the door yielded. Thrusting it open a trifle, she called in: "Lieutenant St. Cyr here. I am coming in unarmed."

No answer.

She went deliberately in. The cluttered little workroom was empty of people. She scrutinized its cabinet-lined walls, its floor, its ceiling, its walls again. No sign of a door to any beyond.

She called loud: "Claudine St. Cyr here. I'm in your workroom, unarmed. Where are you?"

No response.

Again loud: "I am alone. If you are in a hidden room, I am going to find the door and come through. Make your move."

172

Nothing.

Claudine turned the amplitude of the electronic master key to peak volume and with it began a systematic close-range scansion of the wall cabinets.

The last thing she tried was the workbench. Midway through her scansion, the left end of it began to rotate toward her. "Groovy!" she muttered with a hard smile; and she moved behind it and through.

The revealed room was little larger than the workroom; it was cheap-carpeted; its only furniture was a divan that might open out as a day-bed and, against the far wall, another worktable wall-backed by a glittering instrument panel worthy of a space-scouter. Before the worktable and panel stood dignified, facing her, the watchmaker—with the knuckles of one hand resting on the workbench, as though he had just arisen from the chair beside him.

In an ashtray on the table a cigar fumed: from the bouquet, a Sodim e Gomorrh.

They appraised each other.

She asserted: "You are Captain Schwarz, alias Blanchet."

He responded in the watchmaker's weary old voice: "You are crazy, and you are intruding."

He was too intelligent to be talk-euchred, so she played it straight. "You fused your ship and murdered two men and you may have murdered my lover. I am here for one reason: to talk you into defusing your ship. Shall we continue to talk, Captain?"

He said after a moment: "Your eyes and your reason should tell you that I am not the late Captain Schwarz."

Producing the king's electronic cigar lighter, she held it toward his face. "Will you take off your mask, or shall I?"

"It will not be you. If you try, you will drop dead."

"You just signed your name again. Take it off, Captain —after all these hours, it must be sweaty."

A moment longer he faced the muzzle of the lighter as though it were a gun. A wry grin stretched his features.

"I suppose," said the buoyant tenor Schwarz voice, "that it burns off easier than it pulls off. Go ahead."

She activated the lighter. The mask disintegrated. It was replaced by the stunningly handsome blond countenance of Captain Schwarz. But the eyes stayed black, because of the contact lenses.

They considered each other.

"I wasn't quite ready to unmask," he remarked, "but you aren't quite ready to die either, so I can hold you. I am not surprised that you identified me as the culprit— but how did you connect me with the watchmaker?"

"Sodim e Gomorrh."

"I see. I smoked one while I waited in the Gunnery-Aerie; it really didn't matter whether you would identify me, as long as you couldn't find me before I was ready. However, you have. Pleasant cigar, isn't it? The name I give it is sentimental, you know."

"I know. Do you miss Jim Doré?"

"The cigar could not have been the only connection."

"When you put the watch on my wrist and so lovingly caressed my hand, inadvertently you reversed the action of the watch."

"Did I? Dashed careless watchmaker."

Mutually estimating pause.

Claudine told him in a clear voice: "We are wasting time. Save the ship now, Captain."

"As a reward, I suppose, I get you afterward?"

Claudine was ready for this, it was a component in her planning; but now that it was here, she was a little upset to discover that the prospect was not unattractive. However, she held steady: it must not seem cheap, that would lose everything with *this* man! "That remains to be seen," she responded. "You will have opportunity to get me if you can. For whatever relevancy this may have, you were close to winning me the other night in the dining salon; but now I'm afraid we should have to start all over."

"You are confident of your allure."

"Should I be?"

"In most situations, yes. In this one, I am afraid you will lose. My queen is the *Eiland of Ligeria,* and these are

174

holy hours, and I do not intend to go a-wooing elsewhere. My *eiland* is about to die in a famous *bradzh*—must I explain that?"

"No."

"I thought not. This would be a knowledge that you would have used in order to identify me. You see that I respect you."

"That would be prerequisite to approaching me."

"The prospect is not uninteresting. Unhappily I must resist it. My space-empress is *not* going to be disreputably fed into the scrap vats of Ligeria!"

"I am about to explain why you can save your ship without compromising your conscience."

"And I am listening, Claudine, because this is a far pleasanter way of killing time than I had expected."

"The *Eiland* will not be going to Ligeria."

His face changed. "Nonsense. The king purchased her for Ligeria. The new government will claim her. If the king tries to run with her, Galactic will overhaul her sooner or later."

"The king purchased her with Swiss bank credits in his own name. She is his property, so registered with the Galactic Merchant-Astcrine Commission. So he can dispose of her as he wishes. And he proposes to put her into passenger service. Luxury class. Leisure. The life-meanings that you spoke of—"

She was improvising, but it was a totally believable improvisation that might even be true. It had thrown Schwarz into deep trouble, although with his self-command it looked like trifling indecision: he was half-sitting against the worktable, hands gripping the edge behind him, head down, frowning slightly. Wth composure, Claudine seated herself on the sofa facing him: it was no moment to push.

His head came slowly up, his eyes wide, his eyebrows raised a bit, his wide mouth open a little. "You are saying that—if I were to save the life of the *Eiland,* she would continue to rule the spaceways?"

"Until a greater ship is built—and you said that this does not appear likely in her lifetime."

"And Captain Schwarz would command her?"

She looked at him steadily, shaking her head a little. "I will not deceive you. Captain Schwarz must answer for three murders—two actuals, and one attempt which may have succeeded. If convicted, Captain Schwarz will be vaporized."

He grinned openly. "I have committed no murders."

Head down, she studied him under flattened eyebrows. "Explain."

"Swainson: I suspended his animation with a pontine block, just as I had suspended my own. He's alive in deep-freeze, unless the doctors have blundered."

Her head went high. "Hastings said—"

"—that his heart had been inverted. I could do it, but I didn't."

"Why did you have Hastings lie about it?"

"Advanced gamesmanship: you are a challenging adversary, Lieutenant! The golden Ligerian bum got the same treatment: they are both quick-frozen, the doctors can thaw them, the pontine blocks will have worn off by now. As for Doré, I shoot straight: I creased him, that's all: he'll survive. So no murders, Claudine—no murders to answer for. Assault, yes—but not with intent to kill."

"But—their hearts were stopped for a long time before they were deep-frozen. Brain damage, Captain—and gangrene."

"Neither, Claudine. *My* kind of pontine block slows the total metabolism to a point that converts objective hours into subjective seconds. They needed no blood-oxygen: there has been no damage, unless somebody goofed the deep-freeze."

"All right. But tell me why you didn't kill them."

"I wanted them alive for the *bradzh*."

Doubting it, she shook her head and closed with him again. "Nevertheless, you will be vaporized aboard the *Eiland* if you do not save her. And I have taken the precaution of forwarding a full idaradio account to Galactic Police—an account which naturally assumes that they were murders. So if the *Eiland* dies, and you with her, your name will be dishonored just as thoroughly as if you had

176

been convicted in court. And—*for no reason* now, Captain—for no reason!"

His head came slowly up.

"Whereas," she added, "if now you save her, I shall see to it that you bring her into port yourself, with full freedom and command of your ship until you are arrested in port. And if in the course of this freedom you should seek me out, I would be—accessible, although nothing is promised. But if you do not now save her, you and only you will be criminally murdering your *Eiland* who otherwise would continue to rule the spaceways."

His distress was acute, a great fist was slowly beating back against the table edge

Mashti appeared in the doorway and cried out: "Captain Thwartth, conthider yourthelf under arretht!"

Schwarz looked at him, felling him.

Running to the door, Claudine called to the others: "Stay out there! Don't come in! You'll only get me killed if you do! Zhavàr? Brh? Tuli?"

The king rumbled: "Mashti blew his mind. We tried to catch him. We'll stand back, Claudine. You're on your own."

Claudine whirled on Schwarz whose face was blazing angry. She snapped: "That was unscheduled. They were supposed to wait in the street. I have not deceived you."

His fair skin was blood-red. Articulating with difficulty, he told her: "It is almost time for the *Eiland* to die. In one hour it will be too late to reverse the catabolium reaction, and then I will convoke passengers and crew and tell them. In a great *bradzh,* the consorts die gloriously, praising their queen; and so it must be. That was a fine try, Claudine, but it was a bourgeois motive: instead, you should be composing yourself for glory."

Coolly Claudine approached Schwarz, put her hands on his shoulders, tilted up her mouth: "Before you condemn me, I suggest that you taste me."

He took her in his arms. "Cle-ver!" he admired. He kissed her prolongedly—neither hotly nor viciously: deliciously.

He released her. She stepped back, breathing rapidly.

He was trembling. . . .

"No!" he thundered. "I have got to get out of here!"

Whirling, he selected a button on the control board and pressed it. Abruptly Claudine felt weightless and a little giddy. She took a step forward, went out of control, found herself floating in midair.

His hands were gripping her bare shoulders, his face was close to hers. "You are a brave woman, Claudine. I would have enjoyed you endlessly. I might even have persuaded myself to marry you, Claudine. Remember that. Keep that glory high in your mind, just before you cease to be."

He pushed her away and vanished.

Struggling free-floating Claudine comprehended that Schwarz had cut off the artificial gravity, throwing at least this area and perhaps the entire ship into internal freefall. . . .

A pair of male hands gripped each of her shoulders: Zhavàr on one side, Brh on the other. The king snapped: "Good try, Claudine. He got away—probably using PK propulsion, in freefall he could do that."

She demanded: "Are we helpless?"

Brh queried: "You don't know how to handle yourself in freefall?"

She shook her head.

"Then," said Brh, "we are going to take ten minutes to train you, and after that we will chase Schwarz. He can outmaneuver us, but it's all we have."

She turned to the king: "*You* can handle yourself in freefall?"

"Don't worry about me," said Zhavàr. "Get practicing."

25

The technique of maneuvering yourself in freefall is that you find solid anchorage to push off from, and a definite target to attain; and then you turn and push off from *that*, and so on. It is a little like thrusting yourself around under water from one end of a swimming pool, except that you can't swim. Or maybe it is more like putting yourself: after the putt, you are the ball; and if you didn't putt hard enough, you float helpless; and if you putted too hard, you bash yourself crushingly against the target.

The ones who were able to emerge by this method from the clock shop were the king, Brh, Claudine, Tuli, and Gringle. The king and Brh each held one of Claudine's hands for security, but she was doing fairly well. Outside the shop, they paused in midair, searching the star-darkness of Frolic Street.

"No sign," said Brh. "He could be anywhere in the ship."

"I doubt that," responded Claudine. "As far as I know, he has only two control centers for the entire ship: the bridge, and the one in his hideaway. Since the bridge is not now available to him, he will not wish to go far from his hideaway. When the time comes—in maybe forty-five minutes—he will return there to convoke the ship's complement for the doomsday message."

"Then," Tuli suggested, "maybe we should just cover the shop and wait for him." Pause. Tuli added: "I see why that was wrong."

Brh bit: "So where do we look?"

The king sighed. And then he said, very small: "He will be on stage or backstage in Doré's theater."

Claudine reached out and squeezed his hand. "He's right," she told Brh. "What do we push off from?"

The king looked at Brh. The lieutenant jerked his thumb back. The king nodded. Seizing Claudine's hands, he and Brh did a body twist which threw them back to the eave overhanging the porch of the clock shop. From this eave they pushed off. . . .

Claudine found herself on the high place whence eight or nine hours ago she had watched Jim's brilliance. The king and Brh and Tuli were with her.

Midway across the stage, fifteen feet above the stage floor, Schwarz-Blanchet hung brooding. He did not see them, he was half turned away from them.

Claudine whispered: "It is still for me to do. Stay here."

Thrusting off from the platform, she floated silently to Schwarz and locked his arms from behind, saying: "Claudine here. We have quick talking to do."

He held still a moment. Then he told her: "The sex lure was beautiful, but it no longer interests me. Let me alone, Claudine."

"I will not let you alone. You must save your ship. If there was ever any reason to destroy her, the reason is dead now. You must save her."

"Let go of me, Claudine, and go away."

"I will not."

"Then I must kill you."

With a mighty leg-thrust, the king shoved off from the platform and vaulted over Claudine and hit Schwarz in the neck and tumbled with him over and over in midair until they slammed against a backstage girder, leaving Claudine gyrating out of control.

There was a lull, during which Brh and Tuli shoved off and passed Claudine and disappeared in the far wing.

Righting herself, Claudine stared.

The king floated toward her, carrying in his arms an inert Schwarz. Just in front of her he glided to rest with his burden. His lips trembled, his eyes were frightful.

180

After several tries, he asserted: "I seem to have killed him."

Brh and Tuli floated up and flanked him.

The king stared down at the child of his sister.

They let him stare for almost a minute.

Claudine laid a hand on his shoulder. "Your Majesty—"

He looked slowly up at her: still his eyes were wild.

She asked: "Shall we leave you alone with him—or do you wish to help us hopelessly with the saving of the ship?"

He turned his head to stare at Brh.

Tuli said: "I will take care of Captain Schwarz, Your Majesty."

Laboriously turning his head back around 180 degrees, he stared at Tuli. Her face was unbelievably sympathetic.

He handed her the broken burden. She took it in her arms and went away.

Claudine said quietly: "There is no hope. Nevertheless we must try while we exist. I suggest that we go swiftly to the engine room and talk with Commander Suren."

26

On the high place where two days ago they had stared down at the purpling DM-sphere, Suren leaned on the rail contemplating the DM-sphere which glowed now because of its incandescent heart.

Joining him, Claudine leaned on the rail beside him, gazing through the red translucence at the angry, bright violet core. The king and Brh ranged themselves beside her.

Claudine said: "Schwarz did it. He is dead. Again, that is."

Suren shrugged. "I think the reaction is now irreversible."

"If we believe Captain Schwarz, we may have another fifteen minutes before it becomes irreversible. Commander Suren—you are the one man aboard who *might* think of a way. Haven't you thought of *any* way?"

His enunciation was laborious. "I have remembered the way. It is too late for it. Probably it is what Commander Swainson had in mind."

"What is it?"

"We are in freefall, the repulsor-drive is not in use. If we could play repulsor radiation on the sphere, it would neutralize the catabolium by energizing its electrons out of this impacted core and redirecting their electronic spin."

"But you say it is too late?"

"The memory hit me two hours ago. I have a double crew working on the redirection. It will take them another three hours."

"I see."

"But they will keep working, on the chance that the time calculations are off. But I think the calculations are right."

Silence.

"There was a moment," Claudine told Suren, "when I suspected *you.*"

"If it was the moment when Doré was shot," he growled, "you had reason: I'm hot for you, miss, I was jealous as hell. But my mother taught me not to kill."

Silence.

The king said heavily: "Claudine, will you come down with me?"

"Pardon?"

"I am going to try to re-rev these electrons. I may not succeed. To do it, I must lie on my back directly beneath the sphere. It would help my morale to have you lying beside me. Of course, if it blows, we will get it first—but only a millisecond first."

182

"Zhavàr!"

"Explanations later. Allow me to precede you down the ladder—"

27

She lay flat on her back beside Zhavàr, staring up into the angry incandescent core of the catabolium sphere: the sphere's body-blue partially shielded this core, but nevertheless it was blinding. Her retinas were screaming: *Screen us!* She was clutching the king's hand, he was gripping hers.

Breathing heavily, he muttered: "Close your eyes. It's enough to have you here."

"Do yours have to be open?"

"Of course."

"Then mine are open—"

Silence. Heavy breathing.

Her eyes thought perhaps they were being a little less oppressed. . . .

28

There was time now for Jim. She hurried to the infirmary as a matter of affection and duty; but with respect to some other feelings she was curiously cold. Putting it down to tension, she shrugged it off: it would go away. . . .

But as she approached the infirmary, she stopped dead in the corridor. *"Mon dieu!"* she murmured. *"Mais c'est pour le mariage—"* Her brows came down hard. Marry him she could not—it had been a night's insanity, the drive of events had straightened her out, maybe he *had* transposed her. . . . On the other hand, how could she tell him this, when he had convalescing to do? Perhaps he was still critical! Could she *kill* him?

Resolutely she entered the infirmary, remembering that there were other concerns besides Jim. The lieutenant met her. "I have news for you," she told him. "Commander Swainson and the golden Ligerian who was masked as Schwarz may still be alive. Don't touch them —the king will be here any minute to try reviving them. How is Mr. Doré?"

"They may be—still *alive?*"

"For the love of God," she screamed, clutching his jacket and shaking him, *"believe me: I'm a police officer —"* She watched his lips pale. She released him, ashamed; and she grated, fists clenched at her sides, "My apologies, Lieutenant; I am almost in shock, and I did not mean to send you there. Yes, they may still be alive —the king will explain. How is Mr. Doré?"

Coming back fast, the lieutenant asserted: "Conscious. Hell of a headache. Three days rest and restorative treatment, and he'll be better than ever. Come on in, miss—he left word about you."

A moment later she was sitting on the side of Jim's high hospital bed, holding his hand, smiling down at him as he wanly smiled up at her.

He cleared his throat and demanded in a weak voice: "Tell me what happened and who did it."

"Are you strong enough for an emotional shock?"

Compressing his lips, he nodded. "Tell me."

"It was your mentor, Blanchet—Captain Schwarz."

He squeezed his eyes shut tight, and tears oozed out. He was clenching his teeth so hard that his knotted jaw-muscles were trembling.

She waited, gripping his hand with both hands.

Gradually his jaw relaxed, and his eyes came half open, and his eyes gazed glazed at the ceiling. He droned: "I was afraid of that. But I was hoping it was instead my father, even though that would mean he had made me do the things. But I was sure I didn't have the ability to do those things—"

She kissed the back of his hand and waited.

His eyes came to hers. "How about Blanchet?"

"Dead. Really dead. Broken neck."

"What happened?"

"Blanchet re-revved the DM-component to destroy the ship in space, because he couldn't stand to leave her rotting at anchor off Ligeria. Oh, but it was a fine *bradzh* he planned!"

His eyes lighted a little. "He always thought big."

Somewhat chilled, she pressed on. "He faked his own death, and suspended Swainson's animation, and shot you because of jealousy. Tell me, Jim—why didn't he kill Swainson, and why didn't he kill you, when he was willing to irradiate two thousand people with the ship?"

"I understand. He wanted us to be part of her *bradzh*. Go on."

Claudine, very cold now, let her grasp of his hands go lax. "I found him, and told him that the *Eiland* was going to stay in service, and tried to get him to save her, but he refused. In the ensuing hassle, his uncle the king inadvertently killed him. Your Blanchet was about to kill me."

"Where was he when it happened?"

She went even colder. "Hovering above the stage of your theater."

Doré cracked his broadest smile, while new tears came. "He did love me, didn't he!"

"I suppose so." She was distant.

"Then what?"

"The king unexpectedly turned out to have PK. He re-revved the DM and saved the ship."

"I'm not surprised. He taught Blanchet—the fundamentals, and the final polish."

"Oh."

185

Silence.

Jim's eyes wavered away, going back to the ceiling.

No, she could not tell him yet; nevertheless it was definitely definite. It had been a brave dream. It was not, however, the first brave dream that had popped for her. She believed in saving such dreams in their primeval bravery, however false, intact within their own time limits.

"You need rest, Jim," she said, patting his head, "and I have work to do. I'll come back tomorrow."

"Claudine—" Eyes still ceilingward.

"Jim?"

"You're a good kid. I like you very much."

"And I like you very much."

"No, wait. I think I should be blunt about this. We don't have to get married now."

She sat savoring it. Then her ego rocked in a counter-swirling of damaged pride and the splendor of release. She managed to say: "You thought maybe you were guilty. You wanted to marry me so I couldn't testify against you."

"I—guess so." Then his eyes came earnestly back to hers, and he gripped her arms. "But I *was* in love with you, Claudine—I still am! But—not marriage, you see? not yet, Claudine—some day, maybe—"

It was her turn to mingle tears with a wide grin. Leaning over, bringing her face close to his, she told him: "I shall retain the advantage by forgiving you. And I will *not* be seeing you tomorrow."

Her lips brushed his lips, and she left him.

As she passed through the infirmary's reception room, something impelled her to go to the door of surgery and peer through the glass. Zhavàr sat on a stool beside the postmortem tank, leaning his forearm on the tank, peering through the crystal. Behind him stood the doctor-lieutenant, gravely watching.

It had to be important. Claudine tapped a fingernail on the door-glass. The lieutenant turned; Zhavàr did not. The lieutenant came quickly, opened the door, and laid a

186

finger on his lips. She entered, mutely questioning. He closed the door, took her arm, and whispered: "Captain Schwarz is in the tank. For some reason, his life-processes are still with him."

It brought her up psychically short. It constituted a jarring stanza in the tragic poetry of his death, now that he had made his life distorted and useless. She understood Zhavàr well enough to know that the king, despite his poignant remorse at having inadvertently killed his own nephew, was complex enough to be seeing this same point, to be considering the continuing life in a grindingly ambiguous perspective.

Squeezing the lieutenant's arm, she left him and went up behind Zhavàr and stood there. Presently he sensed her and looked around up. He said softly: "Excuse me if I do not stand and offer you my stool."

"Excused, Zhavàr."

He turned back to the tank. "I drove him into that girder with a back-cracking blow. When I held him in my arms, he was limp all the way up and down. He *should* be dead; I say that in an ethical as well as a medical sense. But he is not dead, although I do not know how alive he is. He has an extraordinary talent for survival, my nephew."

She waited.

After a pause, he added: "Perhaps when I hit him and he felt himself barreling backward, instantly comprehending that we would crash into something, he used his abilities to dissociate his vertebrae from his discs. If so, there is a possibility that I can fix him, at least partially. In time, that is. Daily short sessions over a period of weeks or months. I am awaiting the electronic findings to know."

She squeezed his shoulder.

He laid his hand on her hand. Without turning, he asked her: *"Should* I?"

"Why? Because recovery might not be complete?"

"You know my big why."

She considered the subtle problem. Presently she observed: "He has actually killed nobody. He will be disgraced, of course. Beyond that, he will be declared homicidally insane and sentenced to mental cure and then exile. If the cure is successful, he will be able to make a new life. If not—who knows?"

"Can he be psychically cured?"

"He is a paranoid-schizoid personality in a paranoid-psychotic episode. The paranoia can be chemically mitigated, though not eliminated at his age without brain surgery that neither you nor he would want. After that—and some intelligent guidance—he's on his own."

"And then what?"

"You are paranoid-schizoid, Zhavàr. Contemplate yourself."

He thought about that.

He released her hand and returned to consideration of his nephew.

29

In eleven coffee shops and crew rooms all over the *Eiland of Ligeria,* somewhat more than a thousand passengers and crew members were breakfasting when Lieutenant Brh's voice hit the intercom. The others were still asleep; some were awakened by his voice, listened, and returned to sleep.

Brh said: "Now hear this. This is the acting captain. I am afraid I must report that I am still another acting captain. Acting Captain Mashti is the third to suffer a heart attack. However, I have encouraging news: my superior Commander Swainson is not dead after all, he is awake and convalescing, and so is Commander Mashti, although neither will be able to function for the duration of this voyage.

"I am Acting Captain Brh. For many reasons that I will not detail, it is perfectly clear that I am the one who will bring the *Eiland of Ligeria* into port; and I want to assure all of you that I intend not to be stricken—I am considerably younger than those who were.

"Our original destination, Ligeria, is now impossible because of unsettled political conditions. We have therefore changed course and are making for Vash which is, as most of you know, the fourth planet of the star Toliman or Alpha Centauri, the star that is nearest to Earth. From Vash there are frequent embarkations for Earth and almost everywhere else: for those of you who choose to return to Earth, the company will send you home with its compliments.

"Captain Schwarz would be delighted by the following announcement, and I think you too will be pleased. The *Eiland of Ligeria* will remain in space-commission, as the flagship of a merchant fleet which is to be formed by the King of Ligeria. Long live the King!"

"BRAVO!" someone shouted in the first-class dining salon where fifty people had chosen to eat eggs Benedictine. Forty-nine others cheered: it diverted their attention from the two staring eyes Bemelmons.

As they quieted, Brh added: "This is the captain. Out."

Disconnecting, he turned to a thoughtful Chief Tuli. "Somehow," he commented, "I find myself considering it disrespectful to Captain Schwarz that none of them has the foggiest notion—"

There he left it. Tuli had no rejoinder.

Breakfast for Claudine and Zhavàr, in the king's private salon, consisted of champagne cocktails, vichyssoise, beef Stroganoff, and a series of wines. They ate silently.

Presently the king arose, went to the coffee urn, and drew demitasses. Having drawn them, he took a moment to warm his hands on the urn.

Claudine queried: "Were you courteous enough to warm your hands for Tuli?"

189

He paused to look at her, hands hovering near the urn. "It was unnecessary. She exposed no skin."

"Her implication seemed different."

"Evidently you drew the wrong inference." He had straightened. "I invited her in for coffee at about 2300 hours. It amused me to spike her coffee with zac. She has no capacity at all. So I straightened her out on the divan, and covered her with an afghan, and went to bed alone."

Claudine mused: "That is about what I want to do now, Zhavàr."

"No demitasse?"

"Probably not."

He came to her, and gently slipped his right hand under her left arm, and helped her to her feet, and escorted her to the divan, and fluffed cushions, and settled her supine on this couch. There she lay with her eyes half closed.

Her eyes came half open. "Would you take off my shoes?"

Seating himself below her feet, he did so, dropping the shoes on the floor. Then he queried: "The afghan?"

"Merci."

He covered her, and pulled a chair up beside her, and sat moodily contemplating her face.

Brh's broadcast came through.

Silence.

She said sleepily: "I think I like you a little."

"I know I like you a lot."

Her eyes drooped and closed.

For a long time he gravely regarded her face.

Presently he lit a cigar and regarded stars.

She had asked him no questions about the PK ability which he had first denied and then demonstrated by saving the ship at the last instant. Sure that Schwarz had been guilty and was alive, he had kept hoping that Schwarz would save the ship. He had lied to her very easily: well, had she not diagnosed him as paranoid-schizoid? She comprehended a lot, this Claudine. She had asked him no questions: she had none to ask: she comprehended.

190

He smoked quietly, contemplating stars, asking himself what sorts of things he would want to be saying to her when she would awaken.

CODA